Praise

ATHENA'S SHIELD

"Athena's Shield is as meticulously detailed, accurate, and colorful as a Roman wall-painting. Its brave, articulate heroine, the 12-year-old daughter of the rebel slave Spartacus, draws the reader instantly into the everyday life of an alien and fascinating culture, one with problems that echo our own. I have not read a more richly imagined narrative of conflicted teenage experience in the ancient Mediterranean."

--- Richard P. Martin,
Professor of Classics, Stanford University

"Wolf has done her research carefully, so the novel is rich in colorful details that conjure up a vivid picture of ancient Capua and other locations."

--- Amazon review

"A real page-turner!"

--- Judith Rose, M.S.

Also by Lizzi Wolf:

The Versailles of Sadness:
A Novel of Gothic Psychiatry
(2022)

Meager Mercies:
A novel based on the true story
of an 8-year-old boy who spent nine months in
Solitary Confinement
(2023)

Athena's Shield

A novel of the Spartacus Slave Revolt

Lizzi Wolf

Medusa Books
2021

Athena's Shield: A novel of the Spartacus Slave Revolt

Published in the United States by Medusa Books, Tucson, Arizona.

Cover illustration: Detail, fresco mural, Pompeii. This and all other images licensed from Shutterstock.

Cover design by Lizzi Wolf.

A note on dates

The Spartacus Slave Revolt took place from 73 to 71 B.C.E. But the ancients did not consider themselves to be living in *negative* time—"before" anything. Thus, historians sometimes date Roman history from the Founding of the Roman Republic in 509 B.C.E. By this metric, the Spartacus Revolt occurred during the Roman years 437 to 439.

Part I

ROMAN YEAR 437

SPRING

1

Early Morning

I sat in my usual spot, my back against the sun-warmed wall of the women's entrance to the public bathhouse. A sign above my head, scrawled in blood-red paint, announced:

SPARTACUS THE THRACIAN
VS
FEROX THE GIANT

**Two Men Will Enter the Arena.
One Man Will Leave.
Place your bets now!**

My heart pounded painfully in my chest, as if I alone were facing the deadly Ferox, unarmed and helpless. Ever since I could remember, I had felt this raw terror, each time I saw my Pater's name emblazoned on a wall: Spartacus the Thracian.

I had turned twelve a few weeks earlier but felt no different now than I did when I was five and first learned to read his name.

Papyrus sheets posted on either side of the entrance offered rewards for runaway slaves.

THORAX, 15, GERMAN
walks with a limp

GEMMA, 16, A CELT
Missing one eye

RECIDIVIST RUNAWAY
14, Thracian
Branded

I wondered about each of these fugitives. Was there a specific incident that inspired them to risk their life and break away at this time? Were they safely out of the

Roman Republic? Or hiding in a shed in the countryside? Or melted into the masses of a strange city? Had they trekked hundreds of miles north to cross the Alpine Mountains and return to their homeland in Gaul or Thrace or Germania? Or stowed away on a merchant ship and crossed the Mediterranean to Spain or Syria or Numidia or Egypt? Or would they soon be captured and whipped. Or branded? Or executed?

Above the entrance, an announcement in black and yellow read:

DEATH BY DEVOURMENT!
Heraclio the Numidian
Versus
A Ravenous Lion
Don't Miss It!

Before escaping and being recaptured, Heraclio had been *Doctore*–coach and trainer at the Batiatus Gladiator Academy. My pater revered him as a Mentor and I loved him like an uncle. I had rejoiced when I learned of his escape a week earlier and was devastated by the announcement that he had been captured and sentenced to being eaten alive by a hungry lion.

A woman who sold roses in the marketplace knelt to whisper in my ear. An amber pendant of Flora, Goddess of Flowers, hung from her neck. I knew her to be a *villica*, a privileged slave who oversaw the house slaves in one of the many rose, olive, and grape plantations that carpeted the countryside around Capua.

"My child is sick with fever. Please ask the Priestess to pray that he survives." She handed me a pomegranate. "An offering for Dionysus."

"Thank you," I said. "I will tell her."

"For you." She handed me a silver sesterce that featured Cybele driving a chariot pulled by four snakes.

A woman wearing a bronze pendant of Vulcan, God of Blacksmiths, kneeled to whisper, "Please ask the Priestess to divine if my eldest daughter will be married soon." She handed me a packet of incense and a coin of Atlas holding the world on his shoulders.

I nodded solemnly.

A washerwoman with a basket of clean towels knelt to whisper, "Please thank the Priestess for me. My mater died peacefully. I know it was Dionysus who relieved her suffering in her final moments." She handed me three sparrow eggs and a coin stamped with Neptune wielding his trident. On the obverse, Cupid riding a dolphin.

Domina Batiatus sauntered out, fresh from her morning's spa treatment, in which her hair had been washed in aromatic essence, her body massaged with olive oil and scraped clean with a strigil. Filumina, one of her personal slaves, trailed behind her, carrying her bag of bath paraphernalia. Normally, Domina would have been followed by her *ancilla*, a pretty, young slave girl who accompanied her night and day. But, Filumina had whispered to me on their way in, this girl had gotten pregnant and been sold to an olive plantation as punishment. Everyone knew the sire of the doomed child was Magnus, the fifteen-year-old eldest son of Batiatus.

Domina wore a diaphanous silk garment, clasped at the shoulders with silver leopard brooches and tied above the waist with an embroidered sash. A flowing ocean-blue cloak was draped around her shoulders. Her gold Cupid earrings were heavy with rubies, and a red crystal perfume vial in the shape of Venus hung from her neck on a silver chain. Speaking under her breath, she uttered her supplication to Filumina.

Domina Batiatus had known me my entire life. On countless occasions, my Mater had conveyed her wishes and gratitude to Dionysus. Many times, Mater had sent me running across the city in the middle of the night to deliver a salve or tincture or potion at Domina's request.

Frequently, Mater tossed herbs and offerings into the sacred fire, beseeching Dionysus to bestow good luck upon the Batiatus children on their birthdays or in athletic or musical competitions.

"Dionysus loves all women," Mater often reminded me. "The Patrician as well as the pleb. The slave owner as well as the slave."

And yet Domina ignored me as if I were a perfect stranger. The fact that I was the daughter of her husband's most profitable gladiator made no difference. That my Pater's blood had been spilled on the hot sands of the arena in nearly fifty combats to pay for her precious jewelry made no difference.

It was true that I didn't fit into any category of person I knew. I was not a Patrician, one of the wealthy, powerful Roman citizens. I was not a pleb, among the masses of working and poor citizens. And I was neither a slave nor the child of a freedman or freedwoman. Nor was I a foreigner or immigrant, for I had been born in Capua. And yet, while my Mater was a free, non-citizen foreigner, my Pater was a slave.

As the daughter of a Priestess, I was an odd creature by any measure. Except for the Vestal Virgins, most temples were overseen by priests—politicians appointed the title as a mark of status. Priestesses were rare and usually foreign, devotees of foreign gods such as Isis or Dionysus. Few were known to have children. And those few, almost never sired by gladiators.

Even my clothing signaled that I was unlike others. My tunic matched Mater's Priestess robes. Jade-green silk, embroidered around the sleeves and neck in purple thread with a playful parade of fawns, rabbits, snakes, and foxes circling the hem. From a leather strap around my neck, I wore a pendant of a satyr, one of the half-man, half-goats who attended upon Dionysus in his forest bacchanalia.

"Please beg the Priestess to plead with Dionysus that the husband of Domina Batiatus place his bets more prudently," Filumina whispered with a smirk. Any sign of discord between Domina and Dominus was a special source of mirth among slaves. *They may be rich,* the thinking went, *but they are not happy.*

Filumina handed me a packet of frankincense, to be offered to the fire of Dionysus along with the prayer. Domina Batiatus walked off with her chin in the air, as if to demonstrate that she had no worries with which to supplicate the God of grapes, mirth, and women's troubles. Behind her, Filumina rolled her eyes at me.

Women in every state of luck, good or ill, knelt to whisper in my ear. Sometimes they asked me to ask the

Priestess to make them a healing unguent, tincture, or potion, to help them get pregnant or cure a skin disease or make a man love them. Within two hours I had memorized twelve messages and filled my basket with garlands, incense, olives, figs, fruit, eggs, and dried salt-fish.

Late Morning

The entrance to the Temple of Dionysus faced East to greet the rising of Apollo as he drove his golden chariot across the sky. The open-air building was held up by marble columns five times my height. An altar for animal sacrifices stood at the top of the wide steps.

I entered the main chamber, the marble floor smooth and cool on my feet. After a morning spent in bright sunlight, my eyes had to adjust to the shade.

A statue of Dionysus dominated the room. He wore a purple toga and reclined on his pedestal, leaning on his elbow like rich Romans on their couches. In one hand he held a pitcher of wine. In the other, a goblet overflowing with grapes. A ring of fresh laurel leaves crowned his mass of curly, shoulder-length hair. The most striking thing about Dionysus was the mischievous look on his face. I thought of him as the God of Mischief. Of Misbehavior. Of *getting-away-with-things.*

I continued through a narrow passage between two pillars into the *cella,* where Mater stood over a brazier, sprinkling herbs into the fire. The flames flashed purple then orange then green. My senses were overwhelmed by the aroma of burning cedar and balsa wood mixed with frankincense, myrrh, and burgamot.

Mater was taller than most men and wore a jade-green floor-length silk robe. Her red hair, thick as a horse's tail, hung down her back to her calves. Golden sunbursts hanging from her earlobes flickered in the firelight. Ankle bracelets of glass, amber, and seashells clinked and jangled with each movement of her body. Her left arm was covered in tattoos of swirling zigzags, circles, and discs. A green snake wrapped its tail around her neck, its body spiraling down her right arm to her wrist, her fingers closed protectively around its head. Her forehead was marked with a blue crescent moon.

I unpacked each offering and lay it before her, reciting the name of the woman who had given it and her message requesting prayer or divination or offering gratitude. Then I ran back to my spot outside the bathhouse, ready to receive the whisperings of more women, overwhelmed with desperation or overflowing with relief or starving for hope.

"Dionysus is a woman's god," Mater often reminded me. "He lessens our burdens. Fills our minds with dreams of a better life. Gives us reason to hope for the Future."

When I needed a break, I strolled past the stalls selling everything from slave shackles to precious gems to buckets of manure. Above the din of sellers hawking their goods was a cacophony of live animals. Pheasants. Ducks.

Partridges. Turtle Doves. Pigeons. Geese. Flamingos. Peacocks. Pigs. I hurried past them, hating to think they had no inkling of the bloody fate that awaited them in the kitchens of the grand villas on the hill.

The market stalls were bright with rose blooms. Velvety crimson, satin pinks, and crisp yellows accented the air with a delicate, citrusy aroma that assured everyone the season of Flora was upon us. Heavier scents from the perfume stalls that displayed rows of multi-colored crystal vials filled with essences of iris, violet, narcissus, and oakmoss promised exotic adventures in eastern deserts. But nothing could match the comforting aroma of fresh bread, roasted on a spit, that suffused the atmosphere with its warm embrace.

A vendor handed me a hot drink brewed from honey, cumin, and violet wine. I offered to pay, but he waived his hand dismissively.

"Ask the Priestess to put in a good word with Dionysus for my wife," he said. "She is newly pregnant, and we are hoping for a hearty child."

Before the sundial in the center of the marketplace marked mid-day, I had conveyed twenty-four messages and brought enough food for the priestesses to hand out to the sick, old, and poor. A portion of each offering was tossed into the fire with words of supplication to Dionysus, in accordance with each woman's request, but the remainder was distributed to the needy.

I handed the coins to Mater, who used them to buy extra food and medicines for Pater. Allowed to keep one coin, I chose a sesterce with Mercury playing a lute on the face and a frolicking lamb on the reverse.

My duties completed, I was free to do as I pleased.

I ran first to Mercury to give him my daily offering. His shrine was tucked into an alcove in an alley, surrounded by overgrown lilac bushes, the marble statue not much taller than I was. He wore a golden helmet with wings fanning out from behind his ears and a long traveler's cloak and held a shepherd's staff with two snakes wound around it. Golden sandals protected the wings that grew back from his heels. By his side a lamb nudged its head affectionately under his hand. A money bag hung from his belt. At his feet I placed a packet of mint wrapped in linen and tied with a green ribbon.

"Mercury, son of Jupiter, please accept this offering as a demonstration of my reverence for you, God of Messengers, in hope that you will remind your fellow gods on Mount Olympus that the fiftieth gladiatorial match of Spartacus the Thracian takes place tomorrow. And beseech them to protect him from the deadly blows of Ferox the Giant of Herculaneum."

Back in the marketplace, my attention was caught by a dog-eared scroll. The purple wax seal depicted a woman in Greek robes, holding a pen and papyrus sheet.

"How much?" I asked.

"It's yours if you deliver a message to the Priestess for me," the Bookseller replied.

I nodded solemnly.

"Tell her to ask Dionysus not to let my wife leave me," he said gruffly.

At the Temple, Mater said, "I cannot request of Dionysus that he keep a woman in a marriage that brings her unhappiness."

I ran back to deliver her message and return the scroll. I was afraid the Bookseller would be angry. But he laughed good-naturedly and said I could keep it. That it was as worthless as his no-good wife.

A cowbell rang out from the center of the square. The din of the marketplace, called to attention, grew quiet. The slave auction was beginning.

A girl younger than I, in a tattered, grungy tunic, stood on the raised platform, her wrists and ankles shackled. Her hair was a ratty, tangled mess, her feet muddy and callused.

"Ten years old," the slave trader announced. He yanked the chain attached to an iron ring around her neck, as if to liven her up. "Captured during a raid on Germanic barbarians of the River Rhine."

Men jumped onto the platform to poke and prod her. I bristled as if it were my own body being pawed by strangers. She cried silently, her face contorted with the effort not to burst into sobs. A girl who cried openly while on the auction block would be punched in the head to shut her up. I had seen it. Many times.

That could be me, I thought. I wanted to snatch her away from these horrible people. But where would I take her? How could I ensure her safety? The punishment for aiding a fugitive slave could be anything from torture to execution.

"It's not worth it," Mater and Pater had warned me many times. "You would only succeed in getting both yourself and the person you are trying to save killed."

I hated the slave auction. I tried to picture a world without slavery but my mind could not conjure such a paradise. I was pretty sure there was no place on earth that did not have slaves. There must have been slaves a thousand years ago. It was hard to imagine there would not be slaves a thousand years in the future.

The man who placed the highest bid on this heart-wrenching waif was a representative of the House of Batiatus, a slave himself. The girl was jerked down from the platform by the chain around her neck. The procurer handed gold aureii to the auctioneer and signed a certificate of ownership. I elbowed my way through the crowd to tug at the sleeve of her tunic.

"What's your name?" I whispered.

She shrugged and shook her head.

I pointed to myself. "Kalysta," I said.

"Lucilla," she replied, her voice weak and tremulous.

"My Pater is a gladiator at the Batiatus ludus," I told her.

The Procurer jerked her chain, pulling her down an alley. She had to take little shuffle-running steps to keep from stumbling and being dragged through the mud.

At the Temple, I tossed a pomegranate into the fire of Dionysus. The leathery skin turned brown and crumpled. Red juice oozed from the pores and sizzled in the flames, releasing a sweet, fruity aroma.

"The gods cannot hear us if we speak to them as if they were a person standing in front of us," Mater had explained to me. "They live on Mount Olympus, high in the sky. The only way they can hear us is when we burn offerings that turn to smoke and rise up to the heavens to reach them. They can hear the prayers we say over the sacred fire because our words rise up with the smoke."

Leaning into the smoke, I whispered these words to be sent up to Mount Olympus:

"Please, Dionysus, god of foreigners and immigrants, give Lucilla the strength to endure her servitude without sacrificing her spirit."

Then I thought of a better request to make of the god of getting-away-with-things.

"Please help me to help Lucilla regain her freedom."

2

Early afternoon

The papyrus program informed spectators that the lion, fresh from the wilds of Numidia, had been starved for three weeks. What it *didn't* say was that my friends and I had been secretly feeding it.

From behind the Lion's Gate, Felix, Tavia, and I had the best view of the tournament. Heraclio, clad in nothing but a loincloth, stumbled out from a tunnel that opened onto the sands, blinking in the sunlight. The crowd rumbled with uncertain excitement. Before running away and being recaptured, Heraclio had been a celebrity gladiator. At the sight of their fallen hero, they were unsure how to react.

A faint cheer of "Heraclio! Heraclio!" emanated from one section of the bleachers.

These die-hard fans were outshouted by others, who yelled at them to, "Shut up!"

Things got noisier when the people being told to shut up started shouting, "YOU shut up!"

In the cellar below us, the cage sat on a platform mounted on pullies. We stepped back into the tunnel as two slaves pulled the ropes, raising the platform to ground level. The frightened animal emitted a rank, primal odor.

The Dominus of the House of Batiatus sat on a platform shaded by an orange silk canopy, surrounded by his family and friends among the city magistrates and visiting Senators. He stood and raised his palms to quiet the voices still commanding each other to shut up.

"This slave, Heraclio the Numidian, has committed the highest form of treason against Rome. He dared run away from his rightful owner and master."

The crowd hissed and booed.

"Heraclio was recaptured and now stands to face the consequences of his disregard for Roman rule," Batiatus continued. "He is hereby committed to carry out his sentence of Death by Devourment."

"Tear him apart!" a raspy-voiced woman shouted.

"Rip him to shreds!" a bellowing voice called out.

"Eat him alive!" a child chirped.

A pully lifted the front of the cage. Another raised the arched Lion's Gate. The lion, who was supposed to run out and attack the defenseless man, yawned and lay on his belly.

Ten thousand spectators stamped their feet, chanting, "Death by devourment! Death by devourment!"

A burly slave stepped forward from the back of the tunnel, shoving us out of his way to prod the lion's rump with a trident. It growled and ran into the arena. The bloodthirsty crowd rhythmically clapped their twenty-thousand hands. The lion turned in fear, hoping to retreat into the tunnel. But the Lion's Gate was closed. The beast roared, revealing his flesh-tearing teeth. The platform was lowered.

We moved forward along the edge of the open shaft and stood holding the bars of the gate, our faces pressed against the cool iron. The lion pawed the sand in confusion. His mane ruffled in the breeze like sunrays bursting forth from the golden disk of his face.

The crowd hushed. Heraclio stood still as a Hercules statue, staring into the eyes of the wild beast.

Under my breath, I supplicated Apollo, the Sun God whose face the lion so resembled, to remind the giant cat he was not hungry. That he had eaten a bucket of goat entrails half an hour earlier. That the flesh of a man would not satisfy whatever appetite he had left.

I begged Dionysus, god of foreigners and forest creatures, to spare the lives of the man from Numidia and the beast of the wilderness.

I whispered a plea to Hercules, who slew the Nemean lion and forever after wore its pelt, beseeching him to spare Heraclio while somehow also saving the lion. But in any case, Heraclio.

The lion bounded toward the man. The crowd gasped, the expectation of bloodsport swelling them into a state of rabid anticipation. But Heraclio did not flinch. He did not turn and run.

The lion broke into a trot, reared up on its hind legs, lunged forward, and landed its front paws across his shoulders. The crowd held its collective breath, anticipating the thrill of watching a man ripped to shreds by tooth and claw.

But there was no cry of agony. No blood spurted from the man's neck. Heraclio did not stumble. He did not fall.

The lion licked his face from chin to forehead with its giant pink tongue, leaving a swath of saliva that glittered in the sun. The crowd stood in stunned silence, craning their necks for a closer look. Heraclio wrapped his arms around the golden fur of the beast in a reciprocal hug. The lion licked his face again, fell back on all fours, and lay on its belly, looking up at the man with unmistakable adoration.

The crowd gasped in shock. Then whinnied with disappointment. Then hissed in protest. This was not what they had come for.

Batiatus looked about in confusion. He had laid out thousands of gold aurei to fund this event. Thousands more on bets and side-bets. This was not what he had paid for. He raised his arms to hush the riotous crowd.

"Approach," he commanded.

Heraclio stepped to the platform, the cat following at his heel. The top of the man's head was even with the feet of Batiatus. He craned his neck to look up at his former master.

The crowd grumbled impatiently. The lion sat on its haunches and groomed its chest fur with its big pink tongue.

"What is he saying?" the spectators asked one another.

The three of us, crouched behind the Lion's Gate, heard every word.

"Have you bewitched this animal?" Batiatus demanded.

"No, Dominus." Heraclio stroked the lion's head and scratched behind its ears. "After escaping the ludus, I stowed away on a merchant ship. Before I disembarked at the port of Tripolitania, I learned that a slave catcher was waiting for me on the dock. I hid in an amphora, which was rolled down the gangplank and into a warehouse. That night, I sneaked out and ran into the wilderness. There, I hid in a cave. But I was not alone."

"A lion lay collapsed against the wall, groaning in pain. Cautiously, I crawled toward the suffering beast. He licked the paw pad under his heel. I coaxed him to allow me to examine it. A thorn had lodged itself into the flesh. I removed it with the tip of my dagger and poured wine over the wound. The lion licked my hand with gratitude and walked out."

"Later, he returned with the carcass of a hartebeest, which he set at my feet. I built a fire to cook the fresh kill. The lion ate his own share raw, peacefully dining at my side. When I had eaten my fill, I put out the fire and crawled back into the cave. Next thing I knew, three armed men rushed in and threw a net over us. They shackled me and dragged the lion into a crate."

"We were loaded onto a ship. The lion in the hold with dozens of exotic animals destined for hunting games. I was crammed together with newly captured slaves. At the port of Ostia, I was handed over to a slavecatcher, who delivered me to you, Dominus. I was told the lion had been sold to a wild animal dealer. That is how it came to be that this lion greeted me as a friend."

Heraclio's story spread through the stadium.

Batiatus stretched his arms wide to silence the astonished spectators. "This man has recounted a remarkable story of his taming of this beast," he announced.

The crowd murmured in confirmation.

"Set them free!" a woman shouted.

Her demand was echoed as ten thousand voices chanted, "Set them free! Set them free!"

"The good people of Capua have spoken," Batiatus announced. "You wish to reward both man and beast with their freedom."

"Set them free! Set them free!"

"To demonstrate that Rome is as merciful as it is all-powerful, I pronounce that, as of this moment, Heraclio the Numidian and this lion are declared *Free for Life.*"

The crowd roared with approval. Heraclio raised his fists, rotating in a circle to acknowledge his fickle fans. I thanked Hercules, Apollo, and Dionysus and promised to bring them offerings before sundown.

"Long live the Lion Tamer!" a man shouted.

"Long live the Lion Tamer!" the crowd echoed.

Batiatus addressed the Lion Tamer. "Where is it you wish to begin your new life as a freedman?" he asked.

Heraclio looked down at the lion, as if to confer with him. The lion gazed up at him with huge, trusting eyes.

"We wish to return to Numidia."

I gritted my teeth and braced myself for the next event, when my Pater would face Ferox the Giant in hand-to-hand combat to the death.

Late afternoon

The crowning glory of the day's events, and of the three-day festival, was about to begin.

I sat on a concrete block under the bleachers. Tavia and Felix, whose paters, Crixus and Oenomaus, had won their matches during the previous two days, sat beside me. The three of us had been watching our paters fight for their lives from beneath the stands since Felix and I were six and Tavia eight.

This was the Grand Finale of the mid-April games in honor of Ceres, goddess of fertility and crops. Nine days earlier, at the Gladiator games in honor of Cybele, the ancient Mother Goddess, my Pater had won his forty-ninth combat. In May, he would fight in the games in honor of Flora. In July he would fight in honor of Apollo. And in November in honor of Jupiter. During the Saturnalia Festival of December, there would be seven days of games in honor of Saturn.

After the failed Death by Devourment, we had all run back to our jobs. Tavia to baking in the Batiatus kitchen. Felix to chopping wood for the Batiatus oven and furnaces. Me to gather and deliver messages between the marketplace and the Priestess. On my way to and from the Temple of Dionysus, I stopped at the Temples of

Hercules and Apollo to leave offerings of gratitude for allowing the lion and the Lion Tamer to live.

Two hours later, my friends and I met under the bleachers, where we had a ground level view of the arena. Above us, the crowd stamped their feet. After the morning's disappointment with the Lion Tamer, they demanded a spectacularly bloody fight from the star gladiators. Honey cake crumbs and nutshells dropped from between their feet. Wine drizzled down to mix with the mud and trash. This sharp, sour smell was nearly overwhelmed by the stench of urine, this no-man's-land being a perfect place for inebriated spectators to relieve themselves.

In the Arena, the sun had baked pools of blood from the morning's bouts into the sand, conjuring an odor that was part butcher's shop, part roasted boar. The ground was littered with roses and love notes, thrown by adoring fans. Rotting vegetables, hurled by angry men who had lost bets they couldn't afford. Nuts, aimed at contestants by restless boys. Coins featuring the face of Hercules, pitched at the combatants as good luck charms.

"Look what I brought." Felix pulled a wrapped linen from his bag with a dramatic flourish. "Goatmilk cheese with shallots and roasted pine nuts."

At twelve, Felix was short and small-framed. His black hair was worn in thick braids that clung to his head like rows of wheat in a field. He smelled of fresh cut wood and stale smoke. His arms, legs, and tunic were sprinkled with scraps of bark and wood chips. Paint flecks in every color mottled his hair, skin, and tunic. A pendant of the goddess Tanit hung from his neck by a leather strap, a gift from his mater. She had been captured from the Kingdom of Mauritania as a girl during a tribal rebellion and died giving birth to him. His pater, Crixus, was from a Celtiberian tribe in Spain. Like all of our paters, he had been taken as a prisoner-of-war and sold to the *ludus* as a young man.

"How did you get that?" I asked. "I know you didn't steal it."

"The Cheesemaker asked me to paint a mural on the outer wall of his shop," Felix explained. "I drew the likeness of the Cheesemaker himself, dressed as a shepherd, surrounded by a flock of goats, with a staff in one hand and a wheel of cheese held up in the other. In exchange, he promised me a weekly brick of cheese of my choice."

"All the better for us," Tavia said, slicing it in thirds. "It will go perfectly with these."

She pulled three rolls from her bag.

"Did Plutus get a roll?" I asked teasingly.

Plutus was a slave who served as a weapons and armor boy, responsible for outfitting the gladiators during training and in combat. He was fifteen and would soon become a gladiator. Tavia had had a crush on him forever, but only that morning, for the first time, they had made eyes at each other when they passed in the service alley.

"I may have slipped a roll into his bag while he wasn't looking," she smiled coyly.

Tavia, who was fourteen, had skin the color of honey in sunlight. Her hair bounced around her face in large, dark-brown curls. Her arms were muscular from so many hours spent kneading dough. Her skin, hair, and tunic were dusted with flour. The comforting aroma of honey cake, cinnamon, and fresh bread surrounded her like an aura. Her pater, Oenomaus, had been born in Greece, captured as a prisoner of war, and sold to Batiatus. Her mater was a Syrian house slave who died in a plague that swept through Capua when Tavia was five. Tavia had also gotten sick and nearly died.

"From this morning's offerings," I said, displaying handfuls of olives, figs, and hazel nuts wrapped in linen.

Felix sniffed deeply. "Bergamot," he concluded.

My friends assured me they could smell me coming from a mile away because of the heavy aroma of incense that clung to my hair and clothes.

A trumpet blare exploded across the sands. The Trumpeter ran out from a tunnel in a bear mask and bearskin cloak. He pranced around the edge of the arena, blasting his instrument in the faces of those seated in the front row, much to the amusement of their friends.

"Ferox the Giant of Herculaneum!" he announced.

Ferox lumbered onto the sands. The Trumpeter played a series of deep, slow notes, mimicking the plodding walk of the giant.

"Fer-OX! Fer-OX!" the crowd chanted.

His only armor was an iron plate that wrapped over his right shoulder and down one side of his bare chest. In one hand, he held a large net. If Pater were caught in it, he would be helpless, struggling on the ground like a fish on the deck of a ship. Ferox would use his trident to poke and prod his victim's body. To move in for the kill, he would stab Pater in the heart.

"Spartacus the Thracian!" the Trumpeter announced.

The crowd chanted, "Spar-ta-KUS! Spar-ta-KUS!"

The Trumpeter played a string of lilting, whimsical notes that suggested Dionysus frolicking in the woods. Spartacus glided across the sand, so light on his feet he seemed to hover above the earth. He wore a bronze helmet that covered his face, the crest decorated with the head of a wolf, its jaws stretched open, baring ferocious teeth. Like Ferox, he was bare chested. In his right hand he held a spear. In his left a small, round shield. His lower legs were protected by iron plates decorated over the kneecaps with the faces of Hercules and Mars.

A new round of chanting erupted. "Fif-TEE! Fif-TEE!"

My Pater had survived forty-nine tournaments and was the most popular gladiator alive. Outrageous bets had been placed on this bout. *Would this be the end for Spartacus?* The people speculated. Few gladiators survived more than twenty-five combats. Those who had survived fifty were legendary.

I had witnessed Mater's anxiety building throughout the long week of the festival. She had been up all night, throwing herbs, flowers, honey, and wine into the fire, whispering Thracian incantations to protect Spartacus in today's fight to the death. Based on the betting odds posted at the entrances to the bleachers, the consensus was that my Pater had a fifty-percent chance of being dead by sunset.

Tavia clasped my right hand in hers. Felix held my left. My breath came in short, sharp gasps. I felt as if

Jupiter's fist had reached inside my rib cage and was squeezing the blood from my heart. I closed my eyes and crushed the hands of my friends.

"Careful," Tavia said. "I can't exactly knead dough with broken fingers."

"Sorry," I said.

"Breathe," Felix reminded me.

Moments before Pater's previous match, I had passed out.

Above us, the spectators settled in their seats. The fight had begun. I heard the sweeping of the sand as Ferox swung his deadly net in great swoops. Pater would be skipping around him, awaiting an opportunity to thrust his sword into the unprotected left side of the giant's chest.

A man grunted. Someone had been knocked off balance or almost netted. A brief but heartfelt cheer. Whoever it was had gotten up. More sweeping of the net. The audience groaned. Someone had been stabbed or slashed or netted. More grunting. More gasps and groans and cheers. Then a deep moan that sounded as if it had been dredged from the depths of the Underworld.

Had Pater been caught in the deadly net, his chest pierced by the trident? Or had Ferox suffered a stab to the ribs?

The crowd hushed, unsure if the fight was truly over. An eerie silence. Scuffling in the sand. The spectators burst out in deafening applause. Tavia and Felix let go of my hands, the signal that it was safe to open my eyes. Spartacus raised his arms in victory, his foot on Ferox's chest. The crowd went wild.

"Spar-ta-KUS! Spar-ta-KUS!"

My pater had made me promise never to cheer his victories. "A gladiator match is no cause for celebration," he said. "All gladiators are brothers," he often told me. "In public, I must act the part of the proud Victor, to gain favor with the crowd. In truth, if I did not have you and your Mater to live for, I would gladly give my life so that a brother may live to see another day."

Secretly, I cheered inside, each time Pater did not die.

Spartacus disappeared into the gladiator's tunnel. A boy dressed as Mercury ran onto the sands. His curly golden locks flowed out from a winged helmet. He wore a traveler's cloak and winged sandals. Two black snakes were twined around his staff, captivating the crowd with acrobatic gyrations. A man dressed as a shepherd followed, leading a lamb on a leash and playing a lute. Another man, playing pan pipes and leading a kid goat, followed.

Mercury sprinted around the arena, twirling his staff like a baton. The lute and pipe players released the sheep and goat, allowing them to forage on flowers, fruit, and nuts tossed by fans as offerings. The musicians danced a goofy jig while playing a chaotic tune that sent the crowd into uproarious laughter. Mercury spiraled inward until he reached the dead gladiator. As the men dragged Ferox by the ankles into the tunnel, his body leaving a path of blood in its wake, the Trumpeter played a series of deep, short blasts that sounded like Vulcanic farts resonating from the depths of the Underworld.

"There he is!" Tavia gasped.

As the spectators filed out, Plutus entered the arena to rake up the debris and level the blood-stained sand.

I ran to the Temple of Dionysus.

"Spartacus has triumphed," Mater said in an otherworldly voice, without turning her gaze from the fire.

It's hard to explain, but I never cried at the moment during a gladiator fight when I most feared Pater might be killed. Or in the moment I opened my eyes and saw him still standing. I could not cry until the moment Mater confirmed what I had come to tell her. It was as if I didn't believe Spartacus had survived, even though I had seen him standing with his arms raised in victory and seen his opponent dragged away a few yards in front of me. It was only as Mater gazed into the sacred fire and said the words that my sense of relief brought tears.

I believed the fire more than I believed my own eyes.

3

Twilight

On the way to visit Pater and give him my usual I'm-glad-you-survived-another-gladiator-match hug, I stopped at a cross-street shrine.

The bronze Lar was about my height and stood on a marble pedestal. His hair was wild and curly. He wore a short tunic, gathered at the waist with a sash. In one hand he held a stag-shaped drinking horn, raised in a gesture of good cheer. In the other he held out a plate to show that he was happy to receive offerings. He stood mid-twirl on the tips of his toes, his feet encased in calf-high lace-up boots, his billowy tunic swirling as he spun.

The spirit of the Lar was light-hearted. Cheerful. Always in a good mood. Always dancing. Around his feet lay offerings of roses, nuts, quince, honeycomb, dried pears, pistachios, packets of incense, vials of perfume, and charred chicken bones wrapped in leather. A dozen handmade dolls clung to his outstretched arms. I climbed three stone steps to the altar.

"Thank you, Lar, for allowing Pater to survive today's tournament. I offer you this fig as a token of gratitude."

As a god of home, hearth, and travel, the Lar probably didn't have much to say as far as whether a man won or lost a gladiator fight. But he might have some influence in keeping my family together. And for that to happen, Pater would have to remain alive.

At the gate of the walled compound that enclosed the Batiatus villa and Gladiator Academy, the guards greeted me with friendly smiles. I walked across the packed dirt training ground to a low door that led down a stone stairway into the dimly lit cellar where the gladiators were locked in cells when not training or fighting. I was greeted by the rank but familiar smell of sweat and urine from two hundred hard-fighting men. The walls were scratched with graffiti.

Theseus, greatest of gladiators
Thorax, beloved of women
Julius was here!

An action scene in stick figures, drawn with charcoal, depicted a victorious gladiator with his foot on the chest of his opponent. This image gave me a mortal chill. One day, Spartacus would be the man with a foot on his chest.

On the wall space between each cell the names of gladiators who had occupied it were scratched into the concrete. Below each name was a tally of combats each man had won. Many had five, ten, or fifteen. Others had only one or two tally marks to their name. The wall featuring Spartacus the Thracian stood out for the forty-nine tally marks below his name. His fiftieth victory had not yet been added.

Pater sat on a clay bench that was the only furniture in his cell. His eyes were blue-gray with silver flecks. His long orange hair was twisted into a topknot. The hair of his chest was encrusted with sand, sweat, and dried blood. A raven tattoo covered his back, its wings spread across his shoulder blades, its beak stretched up to the base of his neck. Medicus, an elderly Greek slave, was suturing three puncture wounds in his thigh, where Ferox had stabbed him with the trident.

It was difficult to imagine a time when my pater had been light-hearted. He never seemed to suffer from his own wounds, but each so-called victory visibly deepened his sadness. He wore a grave expression on his sun-bronzed face, which was crisscrossed with layers of scars. A long-healed gash ran diagonally from his right temple across his eyebrow and nose to the left corner of his mouth. I was so familiar with this scar that I wondered whether, if it were to magically disappear, I would be able to recognize him.

I was never sure what to say to Pater after a tournament. I could say, *Congratulations!* But to him it was no cause for celebration. It might be more appropriate to say, *Sorry for another brother cut down.* But that didn't seem right either.

I couldn't tell him that, every night, from as early as I could remember, I had had nightmares of him dying a thousand gruesome deaths on the sands of the arena. That, my whole life, I had lived with the fear that he would die in his next match. Or the one after that. Or the one after that.

I wanted to break down in tears. But Mater had often warned me, "Do not cry in front of your Pater. He lives every day with the heartbreak of knowing he cannot protect you." Mostly I wanted to say, *I'm glad you're alive.*

"Keep it clean," Medicus warned, as he packed his instruments.

"Gratitude." Pater handed the physician two silver denarii. "My winnings. Please see that the wife of Ferox is given this donation to help pay for his tomb marker."

When Medicus left, he *shooed* me out of the cell and locked it. Technically, I wasn't supposed to be there.

Pater limped toward me. We hugged through the bars. The cold, smooth iron against my cheeks contrasted with the warmth of his muscular arms around my shoulders and the rough stubble of his cheek against my forehead.

"That lion looked a bit less ravenous than advertised," he said with a wink. "Almost as if someone had been secretly feeding him."

"I know nothing about that," I said, with a look of exaggerated innocence.

"You did a good thing," he assured me.

"The reason the lion didn't attack Heraclio was because they were friends," I protested.

"Friend or no friend, if that lion had been as hungry as he was supposed to be, Heraclio may well have been devoured."

He removed the laurel victory wreath from his head and handed it to me through the bars.

"Please thank Dionysus for my luck in the arena today."

I met Mater outside the compound as she was headed in. After Pater won a combat, she was allowed to visit him. To be locked in his cell after dark and to leave before sunup. The guards kept their distance as they opened the gate, fearing a look from the Priestess could cast an Evil Eye.

To me, she was just Mater. But to others she was a tall, terrifying Daughter of Dionysus. Hulking, muscular men who had killed dozens in cold blood shrank from the sight of the green snake with mystical powers.

At the Temple, I tossed Pater's wreath into the flames and conveyed his gratitude to Dionysus. Tasked with tending the sacred fire, I slept intermittently on my pallet on the marble floor.

"Spartacus has received an omen."

Mater awoke me in the dark with great urgency.

"What is it?"

"Zagreus wrapped herself around his neck."

"What does it mean?" I asked, unsure if I should be excited or afraid. In my entire life, I had never seen the sacred snake wrapped around anyone or anything but Mater.

She sprinkled herbs into the brazier. A pungent waft of smoke overwhelmed my senses. The flames shot up to the domed ceiling. A gigantic green snake danced on the tip of its tail, its body stretched upward like an undulating column. Mater sang a strange, eerie tune in an otherworldly voice. The flame shrank down to its normal height. The phantom snake floated upward and passed through the marble dome into the heavens.

Mater wrote a note in Thracian, using Greek script, on a scrap of papyrus.

"Take this to Spartacus," she said. "Hurry!"

I ran through the dark streets to the House of Batiatus, a path I knew so well I could follow it in my sleep. Shapes began to appear in the deep purple light of the pre-dawn hour. When I reached the gates, Apollo hadn't yet begun his westward journey across the sky. The guards were crouched on the ground, rolling bones in the dirt. These goat knucklebones, shaped into cubes, were carved with a different number on each side.

"Venus!" one of the guards shouted.

His companion handed him a bronze coin and took his own shot at rolling the bones.

"Dog!" he groaned.

"You're here early," the winner said. His breath was sour from a night of cheap wine. Rubbing the bones together in his palm, he opened the gate and returned to his game.

I handed Pater the note through the bars of his cell. He read silently. Then read it again.

"What does it say?" I asked.

He paused for what seemed an eon.

"Is it a good omen or a bad omen?" I persisted.

"*Spartacus will be surrounded by masses who embrace him as a great leader.*" He looked up from the parchment. "Just as Zagreus embraced my throat."

"What does it mean?"

As a prophesy, it was disappointing. This was not new information. At every tournament, Pater was surrounded by thousands who revered him as the greatest gladiator alive. I had expected a revelation more stupendous.

"The true import will be revealed in due time," he said, echoing Mater's equally frustrating response to the same question.

Though I would never admit this to anyone, prophesies always disappointed me. They were worded so obscurely that they could mean anything. Or nothing at all. Then again, Mater would not have called the green snake to rise up from the fire if it were not a sign that something momentous was soon to happen.

I hugged Pater through the bars and took the passage to the stairs that led up to the kitchen. The room was hot, smokey and steamy, the air heavy with the smell of sizzling oil. A dozen slaves were cramped together, their faces pock-marked with burns from splattered oil, their hair heavy with smoke and grease.

Standing around a large marble-topped worktable in the center of the room, they furiously prepped the numerous dishes to be served at the feast hosted by Dominus and Domina each afternoon. A sumptuous table to share with friends, business associates, and rivals was key to their social and political status. Domina and Dominus Batiatus *lived* to impress. They lived for prestige. For Power. For Influence. Serving fabulous food to their guests was an essential element of *dignitas.*

"Kalysta," they greeted me. "You're here early."

"I had to deliver a message to Pater," I explained. "From Mater." Then I wondered if I shouldn't have told them.

A man deboned cuttle fish, ink fish, and catfish. A sea urchin wiggled on the counter. A boy of about eight stood on a footstool, prying open the shells of oysters, crabs, and scallops. He scooped out the flesh, still wriggling with life, and tossed it into oil that popped and spat in a large skillet. His fingers were bloody with cuts from the sharp edges of the shells.

A girl scooped out brains from the skulls of pigs and calves and dumped them into a mixing bowl, her hair sticky with fatty globs. Three women plucked and gutted a peacock, an ostrich, and a flamingo. Two muscular men hacked up wild boar, venison, sheep, and goat carcasses with butcher knives.

It seemed the more different types of dead things Domina served her guests, the more impressed they would be.

Apicius, the head chef, himself a slave, stood over an open flame, simultaneously creating six different sauces that bubbled, boiled, and sizzed in six different copper pans atop a clay stove built into one corner of the room. Apicius was renowned for concocting sauces unlike those of any other chef. He began with a base of wine, vinegar, and honey. Then added secret concoctions of ginger, white pepper, thyme, celery seed, parsley, saffron, marjoram, anise, mint, caraway, cumin, cardamum, fennel, lovage, and coriander.

"See this?" He held a palmful of black peppercorns for me to examine. "Shipped all the way from India." He poured generous portions into each of the sauces. "You know why Dominus must have his ounce of pepper in every bite?"

I shrugged.

"It's like sprinkling gold dust over everything I cook. It assures the guests their host has spared no expense. That every dish is an exotic luxury."

I struck me that each peppercorn had been paid for with a drop of some gladiator's blood.

Apicius leaned close and whispered, "Please tell Amethysta, my sweetheart at Pub Venus, that I'll visit her soon after midnight."

Tavia stood at the table, kneading dough in a wooden trough. She brushed a lock of sweaty hair from her cheek with one shoulder, sprinkled flour onto a board, and shaped the dough. A lion, rearing up on its hind legs, its teeth bared, its mane puffed out.

"In honor of the Lion Tamer," she said. She sketched the face with pistachios, dried berries, and pine nuts. For the mane she arranged slices of dried apricot, emanating from its face like a starburst.

"That's amazing," I marveled.

"Do me a favor," she whispered, slipping a scrap of papyrus into my shoulder bag. "Deliver this to Plutus."

I wanted to grin and raise my eyebrows teasingly. Instead, I nodded solemnly so as not to betray her.

A terra cotta Lar statuette stood in an alcove built into the wall that led to the outer door of the kitchen. A blue crystal goblet of purple wine had been set next to him. A cluster of daisies lay at his feet. A handful of dried pears filled the plate he held out. I added a hazelnut from my bag.

"Thank you, Lar, for keeping my family together."

"We have the best-fed Lar in Capua," Apicius boasted.

I stepped out to the service alley that led between the main house and kitchen to the garden and woodshed. An amber glow hovered on the eastern horizon. Apollo was in a good mood.

Felix was adding the finishing stroke to a mural that illustrated a series of scenes. The lion charging at Heraclio. Heraclio and the lion embracing, the lion licking his face. Heraclio and the lion at the prow of a ship, the coastline of Numidia in the distance.

"Kalysta," he said. "You're here early." In his left hand he held a reed brush with a wool-wrapped tip. He pointed to a wooden pallet in his right hand. "Blue frit. Minimum orange. Rose madder. Red lead. Yellow ochre. White lead."

Each morning, Felix awoke in darkness and ran to the shop of the Pictor Imaginarius to mix colors in exchange for his own supply of brushes and pigments.

"You did all this since yesterday?"

"I've been up all night, working by lamp. This is my first time seeing it in sunlight."

I leaned closer to slip Tavia's note to him. He tucked it into his tool belt.

"For the armor-boy," I said. "From Tavia."

"Of course," he grinned.

A girl approached from the stables, carrying a ewer of fresh milk. She was barely recognizable as the dirty, ragged waif with tear-smudged cheeks I had seen in the slave market the previous day. She had been bathed. Her hair had been washed, oiled, braided, and coiled with a strand of pearls twisted into it. Muddy and gnarled, the true color had been obscured. Now it shone, gleaming like a skein of golden thread. She wore a rose-pink silk tunic, wrapped at the waist with a pale-yellow sash. Her eyes were the palest of blues. A rosy blush glowed on her marble-perfect cheeks. A whiff of Lilac emanated from her skin.

This change in Lucilla's attire and grooming announced only one thing. Domina Batiatus had designated her newest slave acquisition as an *ancilla.*

An *ancilla* was a slave girl whose job was to remain at the side of Domina night and day. To carry her things while she strolled through the market. To stand at attention behind her as she reclined on her couch. To pour her wine and daub perfume in her hair. To fetch a necklace or comb or mirror at the Domina's slightest whim. To sleep on the floor at the foot of her bed. To be awoken in the night and commanded to massage the feet of her mistress or prepare a midnight snack or deliver a perfumed note. To fawn over her with every sign of devotion. Like a lap dog, a pretty little thing whose only purpose was to serve at Domina's pleasure. Dressing her up like a doll went with the role of *ancilla* as a fashion accessory.

"Lucilla!" I called out.

At the sound of her name, she looked up. But when her eyes met mine, I saw fear. She shook her head, signaling me not to approach. Her shoulders hunched and bowed forward, as if afraid of her own shadow, she scurried across the courtyard and disappeared into Domina's private rooms.

I had promised Dionysus I would do everything in my power to make life easier for Lucilla. So far, I had only increased her suffering. On top of everything else, she now had to worry that I would get her in trouble for *dawdling*.

4

Afternoon

That afternoon I met my tutor at the city gates.

Sitting under a willow tree on the bank of a stream, we shared pine-nut-and-thyme cheese, roasted bread, and a quince. Then we settled in for my lesson.

Simon and his pater were slaves who served as tutors to the Batiatus children. Ever since I was ten and he was eleven, he had been teaching me to read and write Greek and Latin.

"I'll give you a coin if you tutor me the way Patrician children are taught," I had offered.

He had agreed but refused to take my money, claiming he needed to practice his teaching skills and that it would help him to reinforce his own learning.

Over the past two years, we had spent countless afternoons under the willow tree. We began with *Aesop's Fables,* written by a former slave, and progressed to Homer's epic poem *The Iliad,* about the Trojan War. One day we would tackle the *Odyssey,* Homer's epic poem about the ten-year journey of Odysseus home from the war.

Each lesson followed the same pattern. Simon read a passage from a scroll. I copied it onto his tablet, marking the soft wax with a reed. Then I read the passage aloud, pressing the wax with the rounded end of the reed to delete words I had gotten wrong and rewriting them with his instruction. Next, Simon helped me to memorize the passage. Finally, I stood to recite it.

"Why must I stand?" I had asked.

"Orators always stand when they deliver a speech."

Simon sometimes recited a passage from Plato, Aristotle, or Socrates. Or pithy wisdom from the ancients. Most of it baffled me. But one thing stuck in my head. He had stood and cleared his throat like a senator about to propose new legislation. He mimed pompously tossing a loose corner of his toga over his shoulder. Then he said:

"Know thyself."

He abruptly sat down. As if those two words revealed fathomless depths of truth and wisdom.

"*Know thyself?*"

"Yes."

"Which philosopher said that?"

"It's engraved on the entrance to the Oracle at Delphi."

"What's it supposed to mean?"

"Do you know yourself?" he asked, looking at me intently. His black hair fell around his cheeks in soft, springy curls. I couldn't help grinning because he was looking at me so intensely, as if it were the most important question in the world.

"I am the daughter of a High Priestess of Dionysus and the Thracian gladiator Spartacus."

He had smiled. Whenever Simon smiled, I couldn't help staring at his strong white teeth.

"But do you know your *true* self? Do you know your strengths of character? Have you discovered your calling in life? Do you know what kind of person you want to be?" He added, "Socrates says the unexamined life isn't worth living."

This conversation had taken place a few weeks earlier, when I had just turned twelve. Our birthdays were a-year-and-a-half apart, so for half of each year he was nominally a year older than me but two years older for the other half. He was now thirteen. But whether our ages were one or two numerals apart, I felt at a disadvantage when it came to philosophical discussions.

"Do *you* know yourself?" I had asked defensively.

"In some ways," he shrugged. "I know what I'm *not*," he said with defiance. "I'm *not* a biblical scholar."

Simon and his pater were Jews. A people who recognize only one God. His pater had been a scholar at the Library of Alexandria, which was said to hold all the written knowledge of the world in one building. He had been hired by the Pharoah to translate Hebrew text into Greek. Simon and his pater had been sailing to Palestine to purchase rare scrolls when they were captured by pirates, taken to the port of Ostia, and sold into slavery.

"My Pater wrote to the head of the Library, explaining our predicament and asking that we be purchased from Batiatus and returned in freedom to Alexandria," Simon had explained. "The Librarian wrote back, claiming they had recently undergone budget cuts and did not have the funds for such a purchase. Besides," he had concluded, "Batiatus was unwilling to give up the prestige of having his children tutored by a scholar of the Alexandrian Library—for any price."

Simon told me, "My Pater insists I devote my time, when I'm not tutoring, to studying rabbinical commentaries."

I did not know of any gods besides the Jewish God who expected their devotees to *read.*

"I am proud to be a Jew," Simon had continued. "And true to my God. But that doesn't mean I want to spend every free moment contemplating Jewish scripture."

"What else *could* you do?" I had asked.

"I don't mind tutoring. I kind of like it. Especially when my pupil is eager to learn."

He looked at me, as if expecting a reaction. It was a moment before I realized he was talking about *me.* I smiled.

"If I can one day regain my freedom," he told me, "I will go to Athens and enroll in the School of Stoic Philosophy."

The idea of Simon leaving Capua made me sad.

"The Stoics say we should guide our decisions based on wisdom, rather than self-interest," he had added.

"I thought only old people are wise," I had said.

"Some old people are wise," he conceded. "It's not their age alone that makes them wise. Many of our elders are as foolish as children. And some young people are wiser than the adults around them."

"How does a person become wise?"

"You make decisions. Every day. Even slaves make decisions. Though their range of decisions is terribly limited. Each time you make a decision, ask yourself if it is the *wisest* decision you could make at that moment."

"At this moment," I had smiled, "I think it would be *wise* for us to get to the city gates before they close and we're left to sleep out in the cold with the jackals."

But I had been left wondering:

Do I know my true self?

What are my strengths of character?

What is my calling in life?

The scroll I had found in the marketplace that afternoon was a volume of poems by an ancient Greek named Sappho. Simon and I sat side by side, each holding one side of the scroll. We took turns reading aloud, alternating each poem. As we read, we unfurled the scroll on one end while winding it up on the other. Sappho's poems give girls advice about fashion, singing, dancing, love, and marriage. Occasionally, Simon paused to consider or reflect upon a specific line.

"*The breeze is soft as honey*," he quoted.

He looked out over the field bursting with purple and yellow wildflowers. Dragonflies with iridescent blue, green, and turquoise bodies hovered over the water, dipping to catch bugs that scrambled across the surface. He lifted one hand, palm up, as if testing the air.

"Soft as honey," he concluded.

In another poem, Sappho praises the goddess Aphrodite for her magnificent smile. Simon looked up from the scroll and smiled at me. I couldn't help smiling back.

"Your smile . . ." he started to say. Then he shook his head, as if regretting he had said anything. His curls bounced around his cheeks, distracting me from his words.

We were so entranced by Sappho's lyrical words that we read all the way to the end without noticing the time. It was nearly dusk. The Bear Guard star was visible in the opal gray sky. We took a shortcut through the vineyards, each running down a different row. When we lost sight of one another, we called out to find each other again. We squeezed through a narrow space between the city gates, just as they were closing.

On the way home, I stopped at Pub Venus to tell Amethysta Apicius would be visiting around midnight.

The Temple was cold and dark. The sacred fire had burned down to smoldering coals. The scent of incense was conspicuously absent. Mater was on the floor, her forehead to the ground. Zagreus writhed spasmodically on her arm. A surge of panic filled my chest.

"Has something happened to Pater?"

Was this the moment I had been dreading my whole life? Spartacus had won his bout with Ferox. But sometimes a gladiator stood victorious in the ring then died later from infected wounds. The puncture holes in his thigh had looked deep. Could they have festered overnight into a deadly blood poison?

Mater lifted her head. The charcoal outlining her eyes ran down her cheeks like black tears.

"Spartacus must escape," she said. Her voice was raw and raspy, as if she had lain there wailing for hours.

Pater was still alive. I could breathe again.

"Escape?" I asked incredulously.

I had often questioned Mater about why Pater did not escape. But she had assured me any attempt would not be worth the consequences.

"If he ran away," she had replied, "what would become of you? And me?"

"We could go with him," I had said.

"If he were killed, trying to run?" she had countered. "Or caught and executed? One runaway slave was recaptured and tossed into a vat of flesh-eating eels."

Her answers had made me despondent.

"We decided long ago," she had explained, "it's more important that we stay together, the three of us, than risk being separated in order for your Pater to be free."

"Pater has never run away because of *us*?" I had asked.

"Most runaways are teenagers," she had pointed out. "With no husband, wife, or children, they have little to lose. Those with families choose not to risk separation as the cost of freedom."

"What if Pater escaped and he *wasn't* caught?" I had persisted. "And we went with him? And we walked a thousand miles. To Thrace?"

"That would be a blessing," Mater had said. "But the other slaves would be tortured to make them confess if they had helped him. Romans believe slaves are only capable of telling the truth under torture. One slave ran away from a Dominus in Rome and the master punished his remaining four hundred slaves by slaughtering them with his own sword."

I was still not ready to give up.

"What if *all* of Batiatus' slaves ran away *with* Pater? There would be no one left for Dominus to torture or execute."

"That would be quite an undertaking," she had smiled.

Now, here she was, claiming Pater *must* escape.

Something had changed. Drastically. Jupiter had shifted the alignment of the stars. Atlas had tilted the world off center. Pluto had rearranged the continents. Zepher had whipped up a swarm of typhoons. Poseidon had tipped the balance of the seas.

I feared Mater had gone insane. It was said some priestesses were in fact lunatics, mistaken for mystics. The wild gyrations of Zagreus seemed a clue. The sacred green snake was seething. Hissing. Her forked tongue slithered in and out of her gaping mouth as if reaching for an invisible enemy.

"Why?" I asked, approaching cautiously.

"Batiatus has sold you to a terrible man."

Now I was certain Mater had gone crazy.

"I am not his to sell," I said evenly.

She beckoned me closer.

"You *are* a slave, Kalysta. You always have been."

Jupiter grabbed my throat and squeezed it in his fist. My knees buckled. I fell to the floor.

"How can that be?" I choked out.

"Because you were born here in the Temple, and Batiatus is the sponsor of this building, he claimed you belong to him. He knew you would be valuable one day."

"Then why has he let me run free all these years?"

"When you were born, Batiatus agreed to allow you to stay with me, because of the value of Spartacus as a gladiator and his fear of my power as a High Priestess. In exchange, I promised to make daily offerings to Dionysus, beseeching him to favor the House of Batiatus."

My face contorted like an actor's mask designed to express *agony*. Tears welled so deep in my soul, I couldn't cry.

"Come," Mater said, reaching out to me.

I scootched toward her across the cold floor and buried my face in her hair, inhaling the scent of burnt cinnamon. Zagreus nuzzled her head on my shoulder.

"Batiatus agreed that you could live free until you turn thirteen. He made no promises about what he would do with you after that. We assumed he would make you a house slave. That you would always be near us."

"But . . . Why didn't you tell me? Why did you lie?"

"We wanted you to grow up free. To see yourself as free. Even after you were to become a slave, at least you would have known what freedom feels like."

"I just turned twelve. I have almost a year."

"That's what Batiatus promised. But a Dominus has no obligation to keep his promises to his slaves."

"Are you his slave, too?"

"I belong to no mortal man," she assured me.

"Where does this terrible man live?" I asked.

"Rome."

A hundred miles away.

My entire childhood, I had believed the only terrible thing that could happen to me was that Pater would be struck down in the arena. That was the fear that hung over me every day of my life. Because of the enormity of this fear, I had never dreamed that any other misfortune might come my way. It had never occurred to me that all manner of terrible things lurks in the future. That there is no divine law that says you only have to suffer one devastation in a lifetime.

"I begged, pleaded, bargained with, and threatened Batiatus. I thought fear of the wrath of Dionysus would persuade him. But he assured me, 'My fear of my creditor is greater than my fear of any god.'"

"Gambling debts?" I asked. All wealthy men had gambling debts.

"He made a bet with a friend over the outcome of yesterday's tournament."

"But Spartacus won."

"The owner of the winning gladiator is granted a substantial sum. But Batiatus also made a side-bet."

"He bet that Spartacus would *lose*?"

"It was your Pater's fiftieth match. He will soon turn thirty, an age few gladiators live to see. Batiatus bet on retiring him to the sands."

Retiring to the sands meant *dying in the arena.*

"Batiatus' creditor agreed to take ownership of you in exchange for forgiveness of his debts," she explained.

"Why place such high value on *me*?"

"The daughter of a high priestess and a champion gladiator brings good luck and prestige to a household."

"When do I have to leave?"

Oddly, I was already thinking in practical terms. Thirteen was nearly a year away. I had plenty of time to mentally prepare myself.

"Tomorrow morning."

Jupiter's foot stretched down from Olympus and crushed me under his heel.

"That is why Spartacus must escape," she insisted. "Tonight."

5

Midnight

I ran through the dark streets, stretching my right hand flat so as not to smear the mysterious symbol Mater had drawn on it with a mixture of ash and pomegranate juice. Of the thousands of messages I had delivered in my life, this was to be the most important.

"In attempting to escape," Mater had explained, "Spartacus risks death. His reason would have to be the threat of a future worse than death. We agreed that, if circumstances were to threaten that the three of us be separated, that would make an escape attempt worth the risk. We decided years ago that this symbol would be the signal that it was time."

"Mercury," I whispered through winded breath, "just this once, allow me to sprout wings from my ears and ankles, that I may live to see Pater a free man. I promise, as soon as I can visit a Temple in your honor, I will make such an offering that you may never doubt my gratitude."

Many times, Mater had told me, "The gods value an offering of a single grain of incense as much as they do a white bull." But in a crisis, I sometimes promised a great offering—just in case it made a difference.

By the time I reached the Batiatus compound, I had made some sense of everything Mater had revealed to me. It had never occurred to me that my life could be different from what it was. The only major change I had ever imagined was the horror of Pater's inevitable death in the arena. I had never once dared to imagine a world where Pater was a free man. I felt as if I had spent my life looking at a wall, without an inkling that there was a whole world on the other side of that wall. I blinked and the wall turned into an open door. Through that door I saw myself, Mater, and Pater. Together. Free. In Thrace.

The guards were slumped on their stools, snoring in unison. I shook one by the shoulder. He greeted me with a sleepy smile and pulled aside the iron bar. Technically, I wasn't allowed to visit Spartacus after dark.

"Tell no one of our plans," Mater had warned me.

"Of course not," I had replied, annoyed that she would think I didn't know what was at stake.

"Not even your friends," she had added.

I wanted more than anything to invite Felix and Tavia to run with us. At least to say goodbye and thank them for their friendship. But Tavia slept in a room crowded head to toe with the other kitchen slaves. I couldn't wake her without rousing all of them. Felix slept in the garden shed. In the dark there was no way I could distinguish him, half-buried in hay, from the other yard-boys.

In the kitchen, I found Apicius removing a pan from the oven.

"Kalysta," he said. "You're here early. Have you delivered my message to Amethysta?"

"She told me to tell you she expects a generous piece of steaming hot honey cake."

"Voila!" He displayed the cakepan, molded to form each piece in the shape of a dolphin.

Lucilla appeared in the doorway. I stood back, resisting the urge to greet her.

"Domina told me to fetch her a honey-cake," she said.

Apicius handed her a dolphin cake wrapped in linen. She scurried into the hall. I followed.

"Wait," I whispered.

"Please," she pleaded. "Domina says I am not to speak a word to anyone. She warned me not to *dawdle*."

I wanted to tell her Pater was going to escape. That she should join us. But there were too many risks. First, someone might see her speaking to me. When word got out that Spartacus had escaped, she would be tortured and interrogated. Second, I didn't know how Pater planned to break out. Or the location where Mater and I were to meet up with him. Thirdly, I didn't think she could sneak away from the foot of Domina's bed without waking her. And the guards would certainly notice Domina's ancilla trying to leave the compound. What if she were killed trying to escape? Besides, Mater had made me lay my hand on the statue of Dionysus and swear to tell no one of Spartacus' plan.

I had vowed over the sacred fire that I would help to free Lucilla. And here I was betraying my own promise. I concluded that this was an example of an *un*-wise decision.

In the future I will not make promises I cannot keep, I told myself. *Especially to a god.*

I lifted the hem of my tunic and grabbed the dagger I carried in a holster fastened to my thigh. Mater had given it to me in case I was attacked in an alley. The curved blade was small but sharp, the handle a green enamel dragon with garnet eyes.

"Here." I thrust it at Lucilla, handle first.

I was afraid she would reject it. If she were caught with a weapon, she would be whipped. But I saw from a spark in her eyes that she had an inner fierceness. Even if she couldn't escape tonight, the dagger might come in handy one day. She took it and concealed it in the folds of her sash. Then hurried across the courtyard.

In the kitchen, Apicius gave me a dolphin honey cake. I thanked him and wished him goodnight. Then I stepped out to the service alley and into the latrine. I pitied the slaves whose job was to be lowered by rope into the hole to scoop out human waste by the bucketful.

I listened through the wall as Apicius cleaned up and stepped outside. His heavy footsteps clomped along the path between the main building and stables, then faded as he turned the corner. I slipped back into the kitchen and placed half my honey cake at the feet of the Lar.

"Please guide and protect every single slave in this household," I asked. "And keep my family together as we travel through unknown lands."

I shoved the rest in my mouth and chewed greedily. On a shelf beneath the worktable, I found the carving knives and roasting skewers. With my shoulder bag full, I took the pantry stairway to the gladiator cells.

The snoring of two hundred hard-fighting, hard-drinking men reverberated through the walls. The floor was sticky on my feet. More than ever, the smell of sweat and fresh wounds and spilled wine and dank walls and rancid lamp oil assaulted me. I counted six cells in on the left and tossed a hazelnut at the dim outline of Pater, who was lying on his side, face to the wall. It hit his shoulder and clattered to the floor.

"Mercy!" he barked, half-asleep.

Mercy! was the word called out by a downed gladiator, hoping for clemency from the crowd to spare his life. It was rarely given.

"Pater," I whispered.

His blanket rustled. His face appeared, pressed against the bars.

"Kalysta?" he whispered. "What are you doing here? Is the Priestess ill?"

I showed him my palm. He flicked a fire-striker and examined the symbol. I was afraid, after all these years, he might have forgotten what it meant.

"Okay." He sighed deeply, as if part of him wished the time for escaping could have been *any* night but this one.

"How will you do it?"

"I will think of something."

Over the months that followed, I would learn that "I will think of something" was Pater's signature phrase. He always did.

"Here." I pulled a cleaver from my bag and pushed it through the bars, handle first.

"Kalysta. What–"

I handed him another knife. And another. He set them at his feet.

"How did you--?"

"I took them," I said, handing him a dozen more.

"Why so many?"

"I thought you might need them," I explained, thrusting an armful of skewers at him.

"Go," he said. I could tell he was already working out a plan in his head. "Tell Mater I will see you at the old well before Apollo has harnessed his horses."

The guards barely grunted as I walked through the gates of the House of Batiatus for the last time. Mater was standing in the shadows, a large basket braced against her hip. She wore a maroon traveling cloak, fastened at one shoulder with a silver griffin brooch. Her hair was braided and coiled at the top of her head. The tip of Zagreus' tail flicked excitedly.

"She loves to travel," Mater explained.

In that moment, I had a flash of realization. Zagreus, a snake, had seen more of the world than I had. I suddenly realized how small my world had been. Capua was only half a mile across. Outside the eighteen-foot walls that surrounded it were thousands of leagues of fields. Mountains. Oceans. Continents. Despite our dire circumstances, I felt a sense of excitement. Adventure. That the future was full of possibility.

Simon had told me he hoped one day to visit the Seven Wonders. The outer reaches of the Republic. The tribal lands beyond.

"Why?" I had asked.

"To see the world with my own eyes," he had replied.

"I have to do something," I told Mater. "I'll meet you at the West gate." I ran off before she could protest.

Simon and his pater lived in a scriptorium built into the outer wall of the Batiatus compound. Inside, an amber glow illuminated a table full of books. I tossed a hazelnut through the open window. It hit the edge and rattled to the tile floor.

"What was that?" his Pater asked.

Simon's face appeared in the frame.

"Kalysta," he whispered. "What are you doing here?"

"I have to tell you something."

"Who is it?" his Pater called.

"Just a street urchin."

"Bring the poor child a hunk of bread and cheese," his Pater said kindly. "And a piece of fruit."

Outside, Simon pulled me around the corner.

"Why are you here? Has something happened to Spartacus? Is your mater ill?"

"Spartacus is escaping tonight. Mater and I are going with him."

"But what of your lessons? We have only scratched the surface of the *Odyssey*. And the Greek playwrights await us. Euripides. Aristophanes. Aeschylus."

Even in a crisis, he couldn't help reminding me of these names, as if reviewing a lesson.

"Come with us. You and your Pater."

"Where will you go?"

"Thrace."

"Aren't Thracian's shepherds? Whom will he teach?"

"Then *you* come with us."

He was silent. It was foolish of me to think he would want to join us. I was nothing to him but a kid he tutored for free.

"I can't leave my Pater," he said solemnly. "Just as you would never leave your parents."

He was right. If Simon were the one, sneaking up to the Temple at night, beseeching me to run off with him, I wouldn't do it. Family truly is the only comfort in the life of a slave.

"Why now?" he persisted. "Why tonight?"

"It's complicated."

"Is it because this was Spartacus' fiftieth fight?"

"In a way."

I didn't have the heart to tell him: *It turns out I'm a slave. I've always been a slave. Batiatus lost a bet against the life of Spartacus and his creditor agreed to forgive the debt in exchange for giving me to a horrible man in Rome.*

"Here."

I pulled the Sappho scroll from my bag. I thought of saying, *Something to remember me by.* But I didn't want him to think I was talking about the love poems.

Simon tilted his head to remove a silver chain from his neck. His glossy black curls beckoned me to reach out and touch them. "Here," he said, handing me the silver candelabra pendant his pater had given him on his thirteenth birthday. "I want you to have this."

"You can't—"

"Yes, I can. *I know myself.* I know what's important to me. I know what kind of person I am."

"What kind?" I asked, feeling dense.

"The kind who gives something that is precious to me to a person who is precious to me." He touched the tip of one finger to the back of my hand. "I will miss you, Kalysta."

I was grateful for the darkness. He couldn't see my eyes brimming with emotion. If I spoke another word, I would break into tears.

Or worse: hug him.

As I ran toward the West Gate, I remembered a conversation we had once had.

"Do you consider yourself happy?" he had asked.

"I guess," I had said.

"But what does it *mean* to be happy? The Stoics say happiness isn't about enjoyment in the present moment. The sweetness of a honey cake. The exhilaration of dancing at a festival. The triumph of winning a sporting competition. Happiness is about how you see your life *as a whole*. The happy man is one who chooses to regard his life as unified by his *character*." He had concluded, "You can't control most of what happens to you. But you can make a series of *wise decisions* that add up to the best possible version of yourself. To regard your past, present, and future as threads in the tapestry of your *character*."

Until that night, I had been content to be a kid. With a kid's world view. Now I yearned to become more than a kid. To regard each decision as a thread in the tapestry of my character.

No matter what happened next, I promised myself to strive to discover my true self. To make wise decisions. To become the best possible version of myself.

Never before had my future seemed so uncertain.

6

Middle of the Night

Mater told the guards at the West Gate she was going to see a sick peasant, to bring unguents and prayers. We walked briskly along Via Appia for about an hour. At an old oak tree, we veered into a forest. Mater strode through the underbrush as if she had night vision. I wondered if Zagreus was guiding her. Based on the thorns and brambles that scratched my arms and legs with every step, we weren't following a path.

It seemed a long time before we came to a dry well at the edge of a field. We sat in the damp weeds with our backs to the stone.

"When will Pater come?" I asked.

I had just told myself I was done being a child. And here I was, behaving more like a child than I had in years.

"As soon as he can," Mater answered, barely disguising her annoyance. "Your hair is a mess," she tsked, combing it with her fingers and rubbing the strands with oleander oil. She plucked violets and clovers that grew at the base of the well and wove them into my braids. "You must be hungry." She pulled a salt-fish from her basket.

"I'm not hungry."

"Eat it anyway."

While I reluctantly chewed on the fish and Mater rummaged in her bag, Zagreus stretched to tap her nose on Simon's pendant. I tucked it inside the neckline of my tunic. I don't know why, but I had always kept my tutoring sessions a secret, even from Felix and Tavia.

"Tell me about Thrace."

"I've told you about Thrace. Many times."

"Tell me again."

"Thracians are descended from Thorax, a son of Mars. For hundreds of years, Greeks, Persians, and Romans have invaded Thrace, razed our villages, and sold our men into slavery. Some Thracian territories the Romans invaded and conquered. Then lost them again, as Thracians rose up to fight for our homeland. Years later, these same lands were reconquered by new generations of Romans. And new generations of Thracians have risen up to reclaim our territory."

"Is our village free of Romans now?"

Our village. The first time I had thought of it that way. No matter what happened after this, Capua would never again be my home.

"I don't know," she shook her head sadly. "Things change so quickly."

"What if we get there and the Romans have taken over?"

"We will join the Resistance."

"Is that why Zagreus wrapped herself around Pater's neck? Because he will one day be a leader of Thracian resistance fighters?"

"Perhaps," Mater replied vaguely. She was always vague when it came to interpreting prophesies.

"What if he doesn't come?" I asked.

"He will."

"But what if he *doesn't*?"

"Spartacus will come."

"Tell me about how you and Pater came to Capua," I pleaded.

"We grew up in a village in the Rhodope Mountains, surrounded by our kin from the Dii clan of the Bessi tribe. We married young, as was our custom. But our lives were torn apart when the Roman army marched in and demanded that the men of our village join their auxiliary troops. If we refused, our men would be slaughtered or enslaved, our homes burnt, our women ravaged, the children scattered. The village chose to take our chances on our menfolk joining the ranks of a foreign army rather than see our homes and families destroyed. As an auxiliary soldier, Spartacus was ordered to march into and terrorize village after village. He soon deserted and joined a band of Resistance fighters. By the time he made his way home, two years had passed. Soon after, the Romans, marched back through our village. They arrested him for desertion and sold him to a slave trader. By that time, I was pregnant."

"With me?"

"Of course, with you," she smiled. "Who else? I packed my basket and followed the caravan on foot. A chain linked each man's neck to the man in front of him and the man behind him, strung together in groups of ten or twelve. We traveled through the war-ravaged lands of dozens of tribes, where they picked up more and more prisoners of war."

"I followed them across the Alps. We stopped in towns and cities along the Italian peninsula, where they sold their captives in the slave markets. In Capua, a procurer for Batiatus bought Spartacus for three amphorae of wine. At the Temple of Dionysus, I was welcomed as a High Priestess. Soon, after, you were born."

We sat in silence. The constellations moved in a steady arc across the sky. With every crack of a twig or rustle of foliage, I expected to see Pater emerge from the woods. Zagreus stretched toward the tree line as if she, too, was watching and listening.

As each moment passed and Pater didn't arrive, a familiar feeling of dread rose in my chest. That feeling when I could hear that a gladiator bout would soon be over but didn't yet know if I would open my eyes to find Pater bleeding out on the sands or standing with his foot on the chest of his opponent.

For the first time in my life, I heard the Fauni, woodland spirits who whispered secret prophesies in my ear. Maybe they knew what would become of us. But I had no idea how to interpret their fleeting, whistling messages from the future.

Rustling and stomping erupted from the woods like a herd of wild horses stampeding through the trees.

"Soldiers!" I cried.

Mater stood firmly, staring into the darkness.

"Shouldn't we run?" I asked desperately.

"I will not run."

I wondered if Mater was overestimating her powers. Or if she had decided she would rather face death at the hands of the Romans than continue to live without Pater. In that split second, I knew I wanted to live—even if it must be without Mater and Pater. Later, it struck me that this was the first truly independent decision I had ever made.

I ran across the field, heading for a copse. When I glanced back, a throng of men emerged from the woods. They burst into the clearing, whooping and hooting. I crouched in the tall grass to get a better look.

I crept closer, staying low for cover. Large, muscular, men with wild hair and bare chests were gathered around the well, gasping for breath. Blood dripping from their arms and chests glistened in the moonlight. Many held butcher knives and skewers. These were not soldiers. They were gladiators!

I found Mater standing among them. I didn't see Pater but didn't want to ask if he had made it out alive. It was clear these men had barely escaped a scene of chaos and slaughter.

Pater appeared at the edge of the woods. He was greeted with a hearty cheer. The gladiators surrounded him with gratitude, punched him in a brotherly greeting, and grabbed his wrists to hold his arms high in a sign of victory.

"How many are we?" he asked as soon as he saw me.

I circled around and among them, counting. "Seventy-five."

"We'll wait here for any stragglers," he announced.

"What about the Romans?" I asked. "Won't they catch up with us?"

"They won't send anyone after us for weeks," he said. "Maybe months."

"Why not?"

"No ordinary guardsman wants to risk his life going up against a throng of gladiators. No messenger will hazard being attacked by us on the road tonight. In the morning, Capua will send word to Rome. The Senators, when they next assemble, will vote on whether or not to pursue us. A minor politician will be appointed. He will have to gather and fund his own troops. Like many great beasts, the Roman military is formidable but slow-moving."

Rustling erupted from the underbrush. Apicius, followed by his staff of kitchen slaves, appeared from the darkness. Tavia wasn't among them. I recognized half a dozen girls and women from the tavern.

"I was at Pub Venus when word got to me of a breakout at the ludus," Apicius explained. "I invited any of the girls who wished to join me. Outside the Batiatus compound we met up with others following in the wake of the gladiators. We made for the West Gate, where the gladiators had killed the guards. It wasn't difficult to follow the sounds of dozens of men, running for their lives. And look who decided to join us."

Apicius pulled a statuette from his bag. The Lar skipped with delight, an impish smile on his clay face.

With Apicius on our side, I thought, *whatever becomes of us from this point forward, we will certainly eat well.*

Someone ran up to me and grasped me in a firm hug.

Felix.

"You made it!" I cried. "I wanted to invite you and Tavia to join us. But I was afraid I would awaken the entire household. And Mater made me swear on the statue of Dionysus that I would not tell anyone of our plans."

"I beat off six guards with a burning log," he said.

"Where's Tavia?"

"I haven't seen her."

"Kalysta!" Tavia stepped into the clearing, hand in hand with Plutus. She hugged me and then Felix. "We're all here!"

"I'm sorry I didn't invite you to escape with us," I said. "I couldn't alert you without waking the others. And Mater made me swear on Dionysus' statue to tell no one of our plans."

"Plutus awoke the kitchen staff to announce that the gladiators were breaking out," she said. "He grabbed my hand and told me to come with him. He unlocked the weapons shed and we handed out swords, spears, and tridents to the gladiators fighting their way out."

More rustling from the woods. A slight figure appeared out of the darkness.

A bear cub?

Wolf?

Cougar?

As it drew near, stepping into the moonlight, I saw a glint of flaxen hair.

"Lucilla!"

She ran up to me and hugged me as if we were sisters. I pulled back to look at her.

"You're covered in blood!"

"It's not mine." She held out her palm, displaying the bloody dagger. "It's Domina's."

A small figure peeked out from behind her. The boy I had seen shucking shellfish.

"What's your name?" I asked.

He stared at me with wide, frightened eyes and said nothing.

We lingered for another hour. Spartacus tasked my friends and I with collecting one hundred and twenty-five clovers. Standing over the well, he spoke the name of each gladiator who had perished in the struggle, dropping a clover into the darkness with each name and beseeching Pluto to welcome them into the Underworld as noble souls who had fought valiantly so that others may live free.

Among the dead was Oenomaus, Tavia's pater.

We tramped through the night, about a hundred of us, Mater and Zagreus leading the way.

I strode beside Pater. I could hardly believe he had made it out alive. That he was no longer a gladiator. No longer a slave. That he would never have to retire to the sands.

I hoped never to learn the details of the bloodbath the gladiators had left behind. But part of me wanted to ask Pater if he had killed the sleepy guards. The ones who let me in without question at any time of day or night.

Who often gave me a date or fig as a treat. Or paid me a coin to fetch them a cup of wine from Pub Venus or deliver a love note to one of the girls. Had Pater killed these young men?

"I invited the guards to join us," Pater said, as if he had read my mind. "They chose to defend Batiatus."

Later, I walked with Lucilla.

"How did you get away?"

"I . . . stabbed Domina."

"How badly was she injured?"

"I . . . don't know. It was dark. It happened so fast. We were awoken by the commotion."

"'Fire?' Domina asked."

"Suddenly I knew the gladiators had broken out and were rioting against the guards. It struck me that this must have been why you were at the ludus so late. And why you gave me the dagger."

"'Go see what's happened,'" Domina ordered."

"Then she, too, realized the mayhem was a breakout. She grabbed my waist and held me in an iron-clad embrace. I felt overpowered and helpless. Then I remembered that Juno once grabbed Diana by the wrists, pulled the arrows from her quiver, and smacked her across the face with them. Diana was like a pigeon, clutched in the talons of a hawk. She struggled to release herself from Juno's grip and ran to hide in the mountains."

"In that moment, I thought, *If Diana can break free of Juno, I can break free of Domina.* I promised Diana I will be devoted to her for the rest of my life if she would give me the strength to free myself. Domina was distracted by a sudden noise and loosened her grip. I reached for the dagger and stabbed her."

"Where?" I asked.

"Wherever I could. She let go and fell to the floor."

"I'll be good to you!" she cried. "I promise! I'll give you my emerald earrings!"

"I was already running across the courtyard. I didn't care if I was struck down by a guard. I couldn't bear another moment shackled to that woman's side. In the kitchen, I heard the boy whimpering and found him hidden on a low shelf. I coaxed him to take my hand. We lingered in the shadows while the gladiators burst forth in a wave, heaving at the gate until it fell open. The ludus was suddenly quiet, except for the groaning of the wounded. I looked down at the boy grasping my hand. I had to decide if I should join them. Or return to Domina with my tail between my legs, begging for mercy. It wasn't a difficult decision."

As she spoke, Lucilla grabbed one of her braids and hacked it off with the dagger. "Only the 'pretty' girls are chosen to be ancilla," she said. She stopped to scoop up a handful of mud and smeared it over her face. "I swear by Bona Dea, the next person who calls me 'pretty'—I'm going to kick them in the groin!"

Whatever Pater and the other gladiators have done to rise up against the House of Batiatus, it was worth it, I thought. *If only to save this fierce, sweet girl from a life of misery and bondage.*

Then I remembered the breakout had been started to save *me* from a life of misery and bondage.

Part II

ROMAN YEAR 437

SUMMER–AUTUMN

7

Summer

Word traveled swiftly that the Spartacus Slave Revolt had been prophesied by a Priestess of Dionysus. Over the following weeks and months, men, women, and children across Southern Italy rose up against their masters and came running to our encampment on the slopes of Mount Vesuvius. Farmhands brought baskets of fruit, hazelnuts, and figs. Amphorae of olive oil. Sacks of grain. Shepherds led their flocks of sheep and goats to the grassy foothills, providing wool, leather, milk, and meat. Children scoured the forests for chestnuts, greens, blackberries, elderberries, wild onions, mushrooms, and edible roots. Teenagers hunted rabbit and fowl. Bands of men and women went into the woods accompanied by a pack of mangy dogs and returned carrying carcasses of stag and wild boar, the dogs yapping proudly at their heels. Apicius roasted their quarry over pits of coals and seasoned it with pungent sauces fit for the gods.

Our band of fugitives was now three thousand strong. The sea of goatskin tents that made up our wandering village was organized into neighborhoods, each with its own blacksmiths, tent makers, bakers, weavers, potters, carpenters, cobblers, and other skilled trades.

I was certain every stray, feral, and runaway cat and dog in Southern Italy had decided to throw in its lot with the Army of Spartacus. Everywhere you looked, they were lurking around, roughhousing, demanding attention, and begging for food.

I came to think of Pater as two different men. To me, he was Pater. But when it came to the Rebellion, he was Spartacus. He even looked different. He had grown thick red sideburns and wore a golden torc decorated with bull's heads.

New arrivals who volunteered to fight spent their days in military training with the gladiators. Many others fell into their familiar skill or trade. And some took the opportunity to leave behind a hated job and seek work or apprenticeship in an area they preferred.

Tavia was working in the mobile kitchen and bakery Apicius had constructed with help from a bricklayer. Plutus volunteered to train the youngest recruits in fighting tactics and weaponry. Felix had grown popular custom painting tribal symbols on wooden shields. And Lucilla had surprised me by joining the archery division.

"I was training as an archer and out on patrol when I was captured during a skirmish," she told me.

Marius, the boy she had rescued from the kitchen on the night of the breakout, had adopted a scrawny kitten. Every day I saw him sitting in the field, playing with his kitten and watching Lucilla train with the other archers.

I found myself greeting children, newly run away from their Domini, who arrived to join us. Helping orient them to life as free individuals in our voluntary community. Giving them a tour of the encampment, assigning them to one of the eight-person tents and introducing them to their roommates.

To pass the time while waiting for new arrivals, we played King and Donkeys, Night and Day, Tortoise, and Triangle near the trail many took to reach us.

Standing in a triangle with Thallus and Anthusa, I dropped a leather beanbag onto the side of my foot and kicked it high in the air.

"Venus!" I called out.

Thallus, a boy of thirteen, caught the ball on the way down with the top of his foot and kicked it up again. "Venus!" he shouted. There was a ragged pulpy hole on the left side of his head where his ear should be.

"You're wondering about my ear," he had said when I welcomed him into the camp earlier that day.

"No," I had answered, ashamed he had noticed me staring.

"Dominus was arranging to sell me to help pay for his daughter's wedding," he had explained. "When he caught me listening in, hoping to discover what my future held, he grabbed my hair and sawed off my ear with a cheese knife."

I had cringed and covered my mouth with my hand, too horrified to respond.

Anthusa, who was twelve, kicked the beanball in my direction. "Venus!" she yelled. Her right eye was a fleshy pink indent.

"Dominus gouged it out with a reed pen," she had told me. "I was pouring wine for him and his friends. He was drunk and wanted to show off what a brutal master he is." She shook her head. "They were not impressed. They walked out in disgust."

"Did they try to stop him?" I had asked.

"They were less concerned with my suffering than with the idea that Dominus had behaved impulsively and without restraint. They renounced him not for his cruelty. But for his failure to demonstrate *dignitas.*"

I barely touched the beanbag with my big toe. It fell to the ground. "Dog!" I shouted, stepping out of the triangle.

Ursula stepped in to take my place. She and her brother, aged fourteen and thirteen, had crept up to the edge of the camp late the previous night, each with a reddish-pink R branded onto their foreheads.

"We ran away when we were ten and eleven but were caught and whipped," Ursula, the eldest, had explained. "The next year, we ran again but were caught and branded."

"As soon as we heard about Spartacus," her brother Damalis had continued, "We ran. If we're caught a third time, Dominus promised he'll sentence us to Death by Devourment."

A boy emerged from the woods, an iron ring soldered around his neck. I didn't have to ask to know the copper rectangle hanging from the ring like a curse amulet was engraved with the name and city of his Dominus. Most likely the back read: Return if found. Reward. He looked terrified, as if he wasn't sure he had reached the right place. Or if I would prove to be friend or foe.

"Welcome," I greeted him. "You have arrived safely at Spartacus Village. You are now a free man. My name is Kalysta."

"I'm Vitalio," he said.

I walked with him to the foundry tent. The chest of the bushy-mustached Blacksmith was covered by a tattoo of a man's body with three heads: a dog's, a snake's, and a lion's. His arms were marked with blue runes. Next to his forge, a huge pot on a bed of coals held a molten stew. He handed me a metal file.

"File at the back. Be careful not to cut into his larynx or jugular vein. And don't file all the way through," he added. "When a thin shred is left, snap it."

While I worked on filing the ring, Vitalio told me his story.

"I was a door boy. Chained outside a glass shop in all kinds of weather. My job was to announce customers during the day and sound the alarm bell for intruders at night. The first time I tried to escape, Dominus whipped me. The second time, he ordered the blacksmith to solder this ring around my neck. I was warned if I ran again, I would be hanged."

There were burn marks where his Dominus' Blacksmith's flame had singed his neck.

"But you ran again, anyway?" I asked.

I was astonished by the courage of these young runaways. Without Mater and Pater, I wasn't so sure I would have risked my life for my freedom.

Vitalio gestured like an actor on stage, presenting himself to an audience. "As you can see," he said with a flourish. "When I turned thirteen in August and learned of Spartacus, I decided, *It's now or never.*"

I snapped off the collar. The skin of his neck was chafed raw. He handed it to the Blacksmith, who dropped it into the vat with a tong. We watched it melt into formless liquid.

"Freedom Porridge," the Blacksmith smiled. "Would you like to pour a serving?" he asked Vitalio.

A clay mold for spear heads sat on his worktable. He handed Vitalio the ladle and instructed him in how to pour the molten metal into the molds.

"Now you have turned your shackle into a weapon that will be used against your former Dominus," the Blacksmith assured him.

The grin on Vitalio's face was incredible. "May I apprentice with you?" he asked.

"I'd be happy to have an assistant," the Blacksmith answered. "But first, you must make an offering to Vulcan." He gestured to a stool with a bronze statuette of the God of blacksmiths, inventors, and engineers.

"I have nothing to give him," Vitalio admitted.

"When these arrow heads cool," the Blacksmith assured him, "you can offer one to Vulcan."

I left Vitalio with the Blacksmith and stepped into the next tent over, where I found Felix painting a shield with an illustration of the moment when Diana broke free from the clutches of Juno. He stepped back to examine his progress.

"For Lucilla," he smiled.

Lucilla's self-transformation from meek ancilla to ferocious warrior woman had amazed me. Each morning she made an offering to Diana, the girl goddess of archers. She pestered a bowyer to teach her to make her own bow. She sewed a sheath from stag leather and gathered reeds to carve her arrows. And she asked the Blacksmith to design a helmet small enough to fit her. Then she approached Boudica, a Celtic tattoo artist.

The masters had done their best to suppress signs of ethnic identity among their slaves. But with their newfound freedom, many now openly identified as Celt, German, or Thracian, as well as countless other tribal and regional affiliations. The tattoo artists were kept busy, decorating the arms of Thracian women with rabbits, fawn, foxes and bobcats, surrounded by circles, dots and zig-zags. Celtic men and women requested tattoos that identified their specific tribe. Germans preferred tattoos symbolizing their gods, as well as mysterious runes they were able to sketch out but could not decipher.

At first, Boudica would not agree to work on Lucilla, because, at ten, was too young. “When your body grows, the images will become stretched and distorted,” she explained.

“All the better,” Lucilla replied. “I will look like a fierce, seasoned warrior.”

Boudica was still reluctant, warning Lucilla she might later regret her choices.

“You may not always want to be a warrior. Best wait until you’re sure of your decision.”

But when Lucilla told the woman she had stabbed Domina Batiatus to gain her freedom, and had therefore earned the right to be tattooed, Boudica agreed.

At Lucilla’s request, Boudica decorated her left arm with blue runes. Her right arm with a series of stick-figure warriors in various postures: Thrusting a spear. Holding a sword and shield. Aiming a bow and arrow. Riding a horse. A three-headed man-monster-god holding a hatchet. On her back, the thunder god Donar, wielding his magical hammer, belt, and gloves.

Lucilla had kept her hair short and choppy--refusing to allow my Mater to even it out--and smeared mud on her face each morning so no one would be tempted to call her "pretty."

"I can't wait to be injured in battle," she told me. "So my face will be scarred."

She had offered to give my dragon-handled dagger back, but I insisted she keep it. Mater gave me a new one with a bone handle carved in the shape of an Egyptian sphinx with blue Topaz eyes.

I hadn't seen much of Tavia since the breakout. When Felix and I were six and she was eight or nine, we followed her around like ducklings. I think she liked the role of big sister. But she had turned fifteen in June, while we were still twelve. She and Plutus now spent their free time with other teens. It was as if she had crossed a social divide that left us behind.

"It's so life-like," I said to Felix, admiring the shield he was painting.

"During the Trojan War," he began, continuing to paint as he spoke, "the goddess Thetis asked Vulcan to create a shield for her son Achilles. He made it with bronze, iron, gold, and silver. On the surface he painted an entire battle scene, with each warrior's face illustrated in lifelike detail. When Achilles rode into battle, the images on his shield sprang to life, carrying out their own illusory battle in miniature. My goal is to paint each shield with such exquisite detail that a person can easily imagine it coming to life."

"You think you can make shields as perfect as Vulcan's?" I asked.

"I can never reach his level of artistic genius and superlative craftsmanship," Felix admitted. "But he gives me a lofty ideal I can strive toward, to motivate me to do my absolute best."

The gods show us an idea of perfection, I thought. *An ideal we can strive toward.* I wondered, *Is there an ideal I'm striving to achieve?*

Felix strived to be the best painter he could be. Lucilla strived to be the best archer and warrior woman. Tavia to be the best baker she could be. Plutus to be the best military trainer. Simon to be the best educator and philosopher.

But . . . *me*? What skill was I striving to perfect?

When not greeting new runaways, I fell into my familiar role of messenger. Running from one end of camp to the other, delivering messages between Spartacus and his advisers. Mater no longer needed my help because women and girls were now free to bring their supplications, offerings, and gratitude directly to the Priestess of Dionysus at her sacred brasier.

Should I strive to be the quickest, most efficient messenger I can be? I asked myself.

There's more to Mercury than communicating between heaven and earth. In doing so, he helps the gods and humans he cares about to live their best lives. As a greeter of newly arrived runaway slaves, I supposed I was helping these kids to live their best lives. Was my role in this world to help others achieve their goals? As a life's mission the idea did not inspire me.

Spartacus had been right about the Romans being slow to respond with military action. We learned from travelers, traders, and messengers our warriors attacked on the roads that when the Senators first heard of the breakout from the ludus of Batiatus, they had laughed. They did not believe slaves, even gladiators, were smart or organized enough to sustain an all-out rebellion. They assumed we would not survive in the wilderness. That, by winter, most of us would come straggling back to our Domini begging for clemency.

In the same month as the breakout, King Mithradates VI of Pontus had started a war in an eastern province that required immediate response from Rome. An uprising in the western province of Spain, led by a rogue general, was also demanding strong action. The Spartacus Rebellion was number three on the Senate's list of military priorities.

We had been living in the foothills of Mount Vesuvius for five months before Praetor Caius Claudius Glaber was sent with a Legion of three thousand to track down and snuff out what was considered to be little more than a riot that had gotten out of hand.

8

September—Evening

I sat high in an oak tree, looking down at the Roman encampment. Across from me, Felix lay sprawled over a branch, belly-down, arms hanging below him like a lounging leopard. Above me, Lucilla was wrapped around the crown of the tree.

The Roman garrison was a picture of order and discipline. The soldiers had measured out ten jugera of fields, five miles from our own camp. They marked the perimeter with palisades and dug a ditch that was also their sewage system. Then they gathered young trees, sharpened the ends, and crisscrossed the trunks like starbursts.

Inside this fortified perimeter, they had marked a thoroughfare with cross-streets extending out from it. Stables for horses and pack mules were built near the entrance. A Command Tent was erected at the far end of the main street, while a flag outside each officer's tent featured his squadron's emblem: Minotaur. Pegasus. Elephant. Lightning bolt. Ram's head. Boar's head. Lion's head.

Like ours, the Roman encampment was a wandering village. Three hundred tents were pitched in a neat grid. With eight men in each tent, we calculated a total of about two-thousand-five-hundred soldiers. Twice the number of warriors that made up the Army of Spartacus.

For the past three days, Spartacus had sent us to spy on General Glaber and his troops. Each morning before dawn, we ran to the edge of the forest to climb a tree and occupy our posts. After dark, we climbed down and ran to report what we had seen. When we returned after the second day, Spartacus asked Felix to draw a map of the garrison on a large parchment that was spread across his command table.

On the third day he instructed us to "Take note of activity that could clue us in to what they're planning." Then he added, "If you see regular soldiers feeding chickens, alert me immediately."

"Why?" I asked. Chickens roamed freely through the garrison, but I couldn't imagine why feeding them would be a clear and present danger to our own people.

"I'll explain when the time is right."

For three days we had heard from our tree-top perches the clanking of hammers hitting nails. Wood being sawed. Deep voices shouting commands. Trumpet calls, signaling shift changes. Men grunting under hard labor. Cavalry horses whinnying. Pack mules braying. Roosters crowing to their hens.

By the end of the third day, the garrison was fully up and running. The rich, tantalizing aroma of roasting lamb arose from hundreds of fires. The encampment was strangely quiet as the soldiers sat gnawing on hunks of meat.

"Ready?" Lucilla called. Her voice, filtered through the rustling leaves, sounded like a bird chirping.

I reached into my shoulder bag, my fingertips touching the cool surface of the stones I had collected. It seemed mean to attack these exhausted men when they had just sat down to eat. But this was war. And these were my enemies.

"Ready," I replied.

"Ready." The voice of Felix, a jumble of husky and squeaky, wafted through the branches.

Lucilla was the first to launch her missile. A rock thumped the back of a soldier's head. He shot up and looked around.

"Where's the donkey-farting arse-wipe who threw that?" he demanded.

His fellow squad brothers, intent on their food, glanced at one another and shrugged. He sat down and leaned into his meat as if afraid someone might sneak up behind him to grab it. I pulled a rock from my bag, aiming for another soldier's back. It landed in the campfire, sending a spray of orange embers into the air.

"What the. . .?"

They all stood abruptly and craned their necks, as if suspecting the stones had fallen from the sky.

"The trees!" one of them shouted.

They shaded their eyes with their hands, scanning the line of oaks that formed a boundary between the garrison and the woods. In our tan, brown, and green tunics, we were well camouflaged. Our bodies swayed in the breeze with the movement of the tree.

"Squirrels," they agreed.

One of them made a fist and shook it in the direction of these imaginary critters. "Shit-eating, anus-mouthed mushroom-heads!"

The men sat down to continue eating, their mood visibly dampened. Lucilla launched another rock. It hit a man's elbow, causing him to drop his meat. His comrades laughed. He plucked it from the ground and tried to brush it off. He poured wine from a flask and wiped the mud with the hem of his tunic. Then he gave up and went back to eating. I winced, imagining the gritty taste grinding between his teeth with every bite.

Felix hurled a stone that hit one of them in the back. He grunted but didn't look around. They had resigned themselves to being pummeled by feisty, invisible squirrels for the duration of their meal.

I noticed some soldiers sprinkling grain at the feet of a clutch of chickens. Then squatting to observe as the birds pecked at their offerings. Throughout the camp, clusters of soldiers were feeding chickens and watching intently as they ate.

"I have to tell Spartacus!"

I scrambled down the trunk and ran up the slope to find Pater.

"They're feeding the chickens!" I told him, still out of breath.

"Call my strategists to meeting."

While we waited for them to assemble, I told Pater we had been harassing the soldiers. I was afraid he would scold me for wasting time in silly, childish games.

Instead, he said, "Good."

"Good?"

"It will make them nervous. Keep them on edge. Always looking over their shoulders. An invisible enemy can be far more frightening than one you can see."

When his war advisers were gathered around his command table, he explained.

"During the First Punic War, a naval ship's sacred chickens refused to eat. Believing this to be a bad omen, the crew didn't want to launch into battle the next day, as planned. But instead of heeding the omen, the captain threw the chickens into the sea, claiming that if they refused to eat, they would be forced to drink. The next day, the entire fleet was sunk. Ever since, Roman soldiers have insisted that, if their sacred chickens refuse to eat, they will refuse to go into battle the next day."

"Fascinating," Crixus said. "But how does this affect us?"

"My daughter has reported that Glaber's men were seen observing as their chickens ate heartily. This tells me they will attack us tomorrow."

I ran back to the oak tree, where Lucilla and Felix were still pummeling the soldiers as they drank their after-dinner wine and tried to impress each other with boastful stories of former battles. Darkness fell. Stars poked through the leaves. The campfires burned down to coals. The men retired to their tents. We climbed down from our perches.

"Let's steal their standard," Lucilla whispered.

I wanted to say, *Are you crazy???* I looked to Felix, hoping he would be the voice of reason.

"I'm game," he shrugged.

Earlier that day, we had seen the sun reflecting off the golden eagle perched on a bronze pole that was planted in the middle of the garrison.

"The standard means everything to a Roman legion," Spartacus had explained. "It's carried at the front of each battle by a soldier whose single job is to make sure it isn't captured. And to plant it in the ground when a battle has been won. In the mind of a soldier, if their standard is seized, they have suffered a humiliating defeat. It utterly demoralizes them."

"Let's do it!" I agreed, hiding my trepidation.

We crawled through the underbrush and crept to the entrance. Three spiked starbursts had been pulled across the road that led down the main artery to the Command

Tent. The guards sat on stumps, gulping wine from a leather flask.

"Wait till they doze off," I said.

If these guys were anything like the guards at the House of Batiatus, the night shift would be devoted to drinking, rolling the bones, and snoring.

Before long, they were slumped together, their arms around each other's shoulders. We crept forward. I shimmied down to my belly, feeling for a space where I could squeeze under a starburst. Then I crawled between the spikes like a lizard. Beside me, Lucilla and Felix lizarded through their own starbursts.

"Lizard Olympics," Felix whispered.

Lucilla and I stifled giggles.

"Mud maze event," he added.

My upper body emerged inside the line of starbursts. I rolled onto my back, sat up, and pulled my legs through. When I stood up, I lost balance and tumbled into the ditch. The stench of manure and urine and rotting garbage made me gag. Lucilla and Felix giggled. The guards snored.

"Stop laughing," I whispered. "This is serious."

They grabbed my arms and helped me to my feet. I dug my toes into the side of the ditch and scrambled up.

Felix scooped up a handful of mud and smeared it over his face, neck, arms, and legs. "Night camouflage," he grinned.

Lucilla did the same. "This way," she whispered.

There were surprisingly few guards stationed among the tents.

"Romans fight planned, organized battles during the day and in good weather," Spartacus had explained. "Inside the garrison, they feel safe."

As we zig-zagged through the grid of tents, I noticed that each squadron had their own shrine to Mars.

A soldier crawled out of his tent and walked a few paces to relieve himself. I was directly in his line of sight. All he had to do was turn his head and I would be right there. I silently begged Mercury to lend me his Cap of Invisibility. The soldier stumbled back to his sleeping pad without so much as glancing in my direction.

The standard stood in the exact center of the camp. Lucilla grabbed it with both hands and, bracing her legs, grunted as she pulled upward. It didn't budge. Felix grabbed it from the other side. Together they tugged, groaning with effort. It refused to move a thumb's-width. I dug around the base with my fingers. When I had cleared a few thumbswidths, they gritted their teeth for one more

Herculean effort. It didn't budge. I dug deeper. No movement.

It took three of us, digging a foot deep until the pole loosened and fell to the ground with a muted thud. We froze, afraid someone had heard.

No one stirred. The air hummed with drunken snores. Lucilla grabbed the pole below the golden falcon. I grasped it halfway down, on the opposite side. Felix took the end.

We marched silently through the dark camp like ants carrying a dead worm.

I awoke with a strange pressure squeezing my arm. It felt as if a leather strap was being wrapped around my neck. Then it moved, undulating like a thing alive.

I sat up with alarm. Wound around my neck, stretching across my shoulder and spiraling down my right arm was a thin, orange snake with bright green spots.

Mater knelt at my bedside. "Looks like you have a new friend," she cooed.

Zagreus uncurled her upper body from Mater's neck and stretched to caress the tiny head of the snake that reached out from my own neck.

"Did Zagreus have a baby?"

"A daughter," Mater smiled. "She hatched in the night and slithered on her own to wrap herself around you."

"How did she . . .? I mean, I didn't know Zagreus had a boyfriend."

"It was a gift from Dionysus," Mater said in her *it's-magical-don't-ask-too-many-questions* tone.

"Where was the egg?" I asked.

"In my hair."

Mater's hair was so thick, I could easily imagine it incubating an egg.

"What's her name?"

"When a name comes to her, she'll whisper it in your ear."

"I hope she tells me soon."

The baby snake nuzzled her scaly head between my earlobe and neck.

"You understand she's a blessing from Dionysus."

"I know."

Why me? I wanted to ask. *Why now?*

As if she heard my thoughts, Mater said, "You've made a number of wise and courageous decisions in the past six months."

"Like what?"

I was pretty sure I knew what she meant. But who doesn't want to be reminded of their own accomplishments?

"You gave your dagger to Lucilla, so she could escape the clutches of Domina. You gathered all the butcher knives, so Spartacus could free his fellow gladiators. You warned us of the Romans' plan to attack. And you seized their standard."

"That was Lucilla's idea," I reminded her. I felt that stealing the standard had been more foolish than courageous and was happy to avoid taking credit for it.

In the middle of the night, our slave army had attacked Glaber's Legion, surprising them in their sleep. In the morning, our warriors reported that, when the soldiers scrambled out of their collapsed tents and saw that their standard was missing, they ran in terror, leaving armor, weapons, supplies, horses, and food behind. But I'm pretty sure watching as hundreds of gladiators drove spears through the chests of their squad-brothers was the main reason they fled.

To celebrate our first victory, the bakers made honey cakes in copper molds shaped like chickens.

It took a while to get used to the feeling of a snake wrapped around my arm and neck, night and day. I was afraid of squishing her in my sleep. Or that she would lose her grip as I ran through the camp. I felt like a mother with her first baby, tentative and insecure about the responsibility I carried for the life of another.

And not just any other. A sacred being.

Mostly I was afraid I wouldn't be worthy of this blessing from Dionysus. Sure, I had made some major decisions that had an impact on the lives of people I cared about. And all of them had turned out for the best. But I faced a lifetime of decisions. I was certain some of them would be less wise than others.

"I promise you," I whispered to my snake, "I will try my best to make decisions that are wise, courageous, and just. And strive every day to be the best possible version of myself."

At night, she glowed ghostly green. I pointed out the constellation of the Snake Holder.

"Once there was a plague raging through Rome," I told her. "The people were so desperate they consulted the Sibylline Books. They were told to send two delegates to Greece, where the sacred snake of Asclepius, God of Physicians, lived. They convinced the snake to go with them back to Rome. Soon after it arrived, the epidemic ended. In gratitude the Romans dedicated a temple on an island in the Tiber River to Asclepius and his snake. The statue of the physician held a staff with the snake wrapped around its pole. To this day, people with every type of ailment travel from all over to this temple. They lay objects in the shape of their afflicted body part at the foot of the statue. Then spend a night in the temple. In the morning, they awaken fully cured."

My snake's spots gradually expanded, and the orange retreated until she was completely green. I found myself whispering to her more and more.

A few weeks later, a new legion, twice the size of the first, under a new commander, was sent to destroy the Army of Spartacus.

9

October -- Morning

Lucilla, Felix, and I were sent down the mountain to wander the streets of Pompeii.

"Hang around the Forum, the public fountains," Spartacus told us. "Wander along the alleys and back streets. Listen in on conversations. Keep your eyes and ears open for clues as to when the Romans plan to send another legion. Find out what people are saying about the Slave Revolt."

He stood with us on a steep slope, looking out across the foothills of Mount Vesuvius. Pompeii was perched on a hill that angled down to the Bay of Naples, where a dozen Merchant vessels were docked. From the Rock of

Hercules, a tiny island in the bay, a colossal statue welcomed ships with open arms. The Sanctuary of Neptune greeted sailors from a wide sandbar.

We cut through fields of grape, olive, and onion crops to Via Consolare, a chestnut lined road that passed through the Necropolis. By the time we reached Porto Ercolano, it was noon. Archers posted on twenty-foot-high towers aimed their arrows at our heads. We were prepared to tell the guards our parents had sent us on a pilgrimage to visit the many temples Pompeii is famous for. But they waived us through without question. Just three dusty, barefoot kids among hundreds of strangers they had allowed to enter the city that day.

From Via di Mercurio we cut down another street to Via Stabiana, a main thoroughfare lined with bakeries, taverns, cafés, houses, shops, and apartment buildings. The streets were crowded with sailors, travelers, foreigners, and merchants from all over Italy and throughout the Mediterranean. The major cross-streets widened into piazzas full of people mingling around fountains, relaxing on stone benches, and making offerings at Lares shrines. It was easy to blend in without attracting attention. Even with a bright yellow snake wrapped around my arm.

Our cover story about visiting the temples was true. None of us had been in a village, town, or city since leaving Capua. Which meant we owed devotions we had promised to our favorite gods during the past six months. Tossing offerings into a bonfire in the middle of the wilderness didn't have the same impact as leaving votive gifts at the feet of a colossal statue.

We headed down Via dell'Abbondanza to the Forum. Felix went to find the Temple of Vulcan, to offer him a figurine he had made of Talos and his dog Laelaps. At the Temple of Prometheus, he planned to offer a bundle of fennel stalks in gratitude for the Titan's gift of fire to humans. Lucilla and I found the Temple of Diana sandwiched between a bakery and shoemaker's shop. Posted on a column was a sign that read:

Runaway Slaves are
TRAITORS
to Rome

On another column:

REPORT
All suspected
RUNAWAYS

And another:

WARNING:
Spartacus the Thracian lurks in the hills
above our great city

More ominously:

Report all suspicious behavior!

"Maybe we shouldn't go in," I said.

"Of course, we should go in," Lucilla scoffed.

"But. . .."

"I'm going in. You can wait here if you like."

I hustled to follow her. Even though she was eleven and I was twelve, I felt cowardly by comparison.

The statue of Diana was caught in motion as she ran through the woods. She wore a short tunic and carried a bow and quiver. A hunting dog ran at her heels.

Lucilla dug into her bag and pulled out a ragged braid wrapped in a string of pearls. Standing at the brazier, she gazed up into the eyes of the goddess.

"Diana, goddess of the hunt and of girls and vulnerable creatures," she began. "I offer you this lock of my hair, which I cut off the first night of my freedom."

The once-golden braid, now dry and grungy, sizzled and curled in the flames. The pearls turned brown then cracked and blackened with soot. Lucilla rummaged in her bag and produced a wadded-up bundle of silk. The pink tunic and yellow sash Domina had made her wear.

"I offer you my ancilla outfit and beg you to protect me from ever again being called *pretty*. I swear, such a fool will feel the sting of my arrow in his heart."

I pitied this hypothetical fool, should he or she ever hazard such a comment.

She unpacked an animal pelt and wrapped it around her shoulders. On her hands and knees, she crawled three times around the base of the statue. After each circle, she reared up and pawed the air, roaring and growling. Outside, she used her dragon-handled dagger to scratch into the stone of one of the pillars:

Lucius of the Zarubintzy
here played the bear
at the sacred feet of Diana

"Lucius?" I asked.

Lucius is a boy's name.

"My name is Lucius," my friend said. "And I'm a boy. I've always been a boy."

"Okay."

As soon as *he* said it, I realized my friend had *never* been a girl. That must have made the dress and role of ancilla especially hateful to him.

"You got a problem with that?" Lucius asked.

"No. . . . I mean . . . The concept of *girl* never suited you in the first place."

"Exactly."

Lucius ripped the papyrus notices that warned the citizens of Pompei against Spartacus from the pillars, crumpled them in his fists, and tossed them to the ground. He sauntered across the Forum as if he wasn't a runaway slave who had just desecrated government signage.

At the temples of Mercury and Athena I gave less dramatic offerings of incense, dried fruit, and nuts.

We met up with Felix at a Thermopolium on Via di Mercurio. The glass-tiled countertop was inset with four steaming pots and a selection of side dishes. Paintings on the front of the counter illustrated the source of the ingredients. A fish swimming. A chicken pecking the ground. Grapes on the vine. A mouse nibling on a grain of wheat. Bees buzzing around a hive.

Four men in togas sat at a table.

"I guarantee," one man was saying, "when I am elected Magistrate, Pompeii need never fear a gladiator uprising—nor any slave rebellion."

We froze in our tracks.

"How do you presume to accomplish such a feat?" one of his companions asked.

"I know slaves. I know how their puny minds work. What makes their hearts beat. They must always fear the consequences of running away more than anything they endure under the yoke of their Domini."

"You call for gentler treatment of slaves?" asked another.

"Much the opposite. I propose the city pass an ordinance, guaranteeing that any slave who attempts to run be immediately executed in the Forum. Side by side with six of their companions from the same household. No second chances."

"That would be an expensive law for the average Dominus to honor. Slaves are cheap. But not that cheap."

"My proposal includes municipal subsidies to reimburse affected Domini for replacement slaves."

"Wouldn't that place quite a burden on city taxpayers?"

"Not at all. With a law this stringent, no slave will ever *dream* of escaping."

I wanted to shout in their faces, *There's no such thing as a slave who doesn't dream of escaping!*

The server stepped into the kitchen with an empty pot. The politician raised his glass and glanced around.

"You!" he called.

We eyed each other nervously. If he assumed we were slaves, would he ask the name of our Dominus? Would he suspect we had wandered down from the mountain occupied by Spartacus and his band of runaways?

"Boy!" the politician barked.

He could have meant Lucius or Felix. There was nothing about Lucius that would make a stranger think he had ever been considered a girl.

Felix stepped forward.

"Wine!" the politician demanded.

"Yes, Dominus." Felix stepped behind the counter to get the wine, almost colliding with the server, who was returning from the kitchen with a pot of hot lentils.

"Get out of my way!" he scolded. "What is wrong with you?"

Felix pointed to the politician. "That table would like more wine."

"Here," the server thrust a pitcher at him.

"But I don't—" Felix protested.

"Do you and your pals want me to kick you out to the gutter?" the server asked.

Felix shook his head.

"Then pour the man's wine."

The politician was holding his glass above and slightly behind his own head. It wavered in the air. Felix's hands tremored as he aimed the pitcher's flow into the narrow glass. Wine spilled to the floor at his feet.

"Donkey-headed fool!" The server grabbed the pitcher, circled the table, and filled each man's glass without spilling a drop. "This round is on the house," he assured them.

As it turned out, three kids in plain tunics, no different from those worn by the children of peasants, freedmen, shopkeepers, and traders, were not worth scrutinizing. Besides assuming Felix was there to serve them, these rich, powerful men paid no more attention to us than they would a stray dog wandering in from the alley.

I handed the server three coins. He grabbed three tin plates from a stack and piled each with baked cheese, poppyseed bread, deep-fried sardines, roasted turnips, purple grapes, and a side of garum. He poured each of us a warm, syrupy fruit drink, then handed me a side dish with a deep-fried dormouse dipped in honey and rolled in poppyseeds.

"For her." He winked at the snake on my arm. "For luck."

To my surprise, my snake winked back.

We were directed down a short passageway to the back room. "Where the plebs sit." The atmosphere resembled the raucous, noisy tumult of a tavern. Crowded around small tables, seated on benches, and leaning against walls were sailors, soldiers, slaves, tradesmen, peasants, and vendors. I overheard people speaking Oscan, Greek, Latin, and a handful of languages I didn't recognize. We sat on a clay bench built into the wall. A mural above our heads illustrated stages in a fistfight over the outcome of a roll of the bones that progressed into an all-out brawl spilling into the alley.

I held out the dormouse for my snake, who unhinged her jaw to begin the long process of swallowing it whole. We ate quietly, looking down at our plates while perking up our ears for any talk of the Spartacus Revolt or the Roman Army's plans to pursue us. It didn't take long.

". . . *Spartacus* . . ."

We all heard it.

"What did they say about him?" I mumbled with a mouthful of lentils.

"I don't know," Felix mumbled back. "All I heard was his name."

"Same here," Lucius shrugged.

And again. ". . . *Spartacus* . . ."

". . . *Spartacus* . . ."

The name Spartacus was on everyone's lips. But in the hustle and bustle of the crowded café, it was impossible to catch the gist of what was being said about him.

After our meal, we split up to wander through the streets. I stepped into a Scriptorium on Via del Fortuna. The shelves were filled with scrolls organized by subject. Literature. Philosophy. Mathematics. Medicine. A scribe sat behind the counter, copying text from one scroll onto another. His hair was dark and curly.

"Excuse me. Do you have any copies of *The Voyage of Jason and the Argonauts*?" I asked.

He looked up. Our eyes met. Too stunned to speak.

"Kalysta?"

"Simon?"

Both at the same time: "What are you doing here?"

Simon stepped to the front of the counter. Before I knew it, we were hugging. Then whispering.

"I thought you ran away with Spartacus."

"I thought you stayed in Capua with your pater."

"Seriously. What are you doing in Pompeii?" Simon asked.

"We're camped on Mount Vesuvius. Three-thousand of us."

"I heard about that. But I didn't know so many had joined you."

"Pater sent me here with Lucius and Felix to find out what people are saying about the Rebellion. And when Rome plans to send another Legion. What are *you* doing in Pompeii?"

"After the breakout, there was a crackdown on slaves in Capua."

"Was anyone executed?"

"The Domini were afraid of another uprising if they punished the remaining slaves too harshly. They praised those who had not run away with Spartacus for their loyalty. They put tighter restrictions on the movement and activities of slaves. Increased the number of paid snitches. My Pater thought it best for me to leave for a while, until things settle down. He sent me to Pompeii, with Batiatus' permission, on the pretext of copying rare scrolls from the Bookseller here. He's Jewish, too. I'm sharing a room with his sons. And who is this?"

Since entering the shop, my snake had sprouted purple spots on her yellow skin.

"Zagreus had a baby. It's her daughter."

"What's her name?"

"She hasn't told me yet. Mater says when she's ready, she'll whisper it in my ear."

I felt foolish, just standing there looking at each other. I remembered that he had turned fourteen in September, so I said, "Happy birthday."

"Thanks."

"Was your Pater angry with you for giving away your pendant?"

"At first," Simon nodded vigorously. "He noticed right away, the morning after the breakout. I was tempted to lie and said I had lost it. But I chose to tell the truth. He was deeply disappointed. 'Couldn't you have given her something else?' he asked. 'That was your grandfather's. I had hoped you would one day give it to your son.'"

"You ought to keep it," I assured him. "To honor your family."

I removed the pendant and gave it to him. He hung it around his own neck. My snake stretched to tap the silver candelabra with her nose, as if bidding it goodbye or confirming that it had again found its proper home.

"Maybe that's why your god fated us to meet again," I suggested. "So I could return your family heirloom."

"I'm not so sure the Jewish God operates at that level. Come with me." He led me through the aisles to a section labelled Literature: Greek, pulled a scroll from the shelf, and handed it to me.

I read the wax seal. "*Jason and the Argonauts.* Apollonius of Rhodes. Thank you!"

"Will you be here tonight?" he asked brightly. "We should go to the theatre."

10

Evening

Simon led us down Via Stabiana to the Theatre, an open-air playhouse with a semi-circle of stone bleachers built into the side of a hill. I recognized the politician and his friends sitting in the front row. Part of me thought the presence of these enemies of Freedom should dampen my mood. But I was too excited to be seeing famous actors like Metrobius and Roscius live on stage to let it ruin my night. And the lead was to be played by Cytheris.

The play was called *Antigone*. Simon told me it was written by an ancient Greek named Sophocles. It opens with the Chorus chanting an explanation of events that took place in the city of Thebes before the first scene.

Two brothers, nephews of the King, started a civil war against each other over which of them would become the next king. After a long and bloody war, the brothers slew each other outside the city gates. Their uncle, the King of Thebes, declared that one of the brothers was a hero. He was given a hero's funeral, with a procession, cremation on a bier, and all the ritual required by the gods for a person's soul to pass into the Underworld. The King declared the other brother to be a traitor. He decreed that his corpse be left to rot in the sun, his bones picked bare by vultures. Anyone caught performing funeral rites over his body would be executed.

In the first scene, the sisters of the slain rivals are talking. Antigone tells her sister she plans to sneak outside the city walls to perform funeral rites for the brother who was declared a traitor. She invites her sister to join her. But her sister says she doesn't want to break the law. Antigone tells her some laws are greater than the laws of man. That properly burying their brother is the *right thing to do.* And the *right* thing isn't always the *legal* thing. Laws are made by men. But the greater laws of Justice are determined by higher powers.

Antigone is arrested for burying her brother and brought before the King. The Chorus, who represent the thoughts and feelings of the common people, beg and plead with him not to put her to death. Everyone understands why she did what she did. That it was the *right thing* for a girl to do for her brother. They forgive her for breaking the King's law in order to obey the laws of the gods. Even his own son, who is engaged to Antigone, begs for clemency. But the King fears he'll be seen as weak and feminine if he doesn't enforce his own law. Antigone is taken in shackles to a cave, where she is sealed in with a boulder and left to die in darkness.

After the play, we bought cassata, a ricotta-cheese cake with red almond paste crust and candied fruit on top, eaten with a spoon, and sat at a fountain to enjoy our treat.

"If you were in Thebes at the time of Antigone," Simon asked, "what would you have done?"

"Assassinated King Creon and placed Antigone on the throne," Lucius answered.

"I would paint murals throughout the city," Felix said, "of Antigone pouring libations over her brother's body. And the words: FREE ANTIGONE!"

"I would use philosophy to convince the King that, in order to live a good life, he would have to make a wise and just decision: to free Antigone and publicly acknowledge that she had done the right thing in obeying her gods," Simon said.

They all looked at me.

"I would probably be that messenger who informs Creon that Antigone has defied him. Then begs the King not to punish him for being the bearer of bad news."

"Don't kill the messenger!" Simon grinned.

We all laughed.

"Oh, come on, Kalysta!" Lucius burst out. "You totally would have helped Antigone bury her brother."

"Then helped her to escape," Simon added.

"Shhh!" Felix hissed. He gestured to a young couple sitting near us.

"Antigone is like Spartacus," the woman commented. "She obeyed the laws of the gods in defiance of the laws of man."

"And look how she was rewarded?" her companion said. "Sealed in a cave to starve to death."

"Unlike Antigone," the woman countered, "Spartacus has not been caught."

"*Yet,*" the man noted.

"You *want* him to be caught?" she asked. She looked around and whispered conspiratorially in his ear.

More and more I was getting the impression there was an undercurrent of people in Pompeii sympathetic to the Spartacus Revolt.

It was late. Simon told the Book Seller he had run into some old friends at the theatre and asked if we could sleep on the floor of the shop.

"Only if they arrive after midnight and are gone by sunup," the Book Seller told him. He must have known we were runaways. But he said nothing.

We entered the Scriptorium from an alley through the back door and lay on pallets between the shelves.

Morning

A feather brushed across my ear. . .. *Antigone* . . .

. . . a childlike voice wafted into my consciousness on a gentle breeze from far away. . .. *Antigone* . . .

My snake was tickling my ear with her tongue. During the night she had turned turquoise, the color worn by Antigone in the play.

"Antigone," I said. "That's your name!"

She tapped the underside of my chin with the top of her head. I sat up and looked around. Felix's pallet had been rolled up and set behind the counter. He must have woken early and gone out to explore. Lucius was still sleeping.

"Lucius." I shook him awake. "Guess what? My snake told me her name is Antigone."

"That's perfect for her," Lucius said, rubbing sleep from his eyes.

Antigone stretched toward him. He petted the top of her scaly head with his finger.

We bought warm flatbread with honey, nuts, and dates from a street vender and sat at a cross-street fountain to eat. Afterword, we wandered down alleys and backstreets, keeping our eyes and ears tuned. So far, we had failed to learn any information about the next attack planned against Spartacus.

From Via dell'Abbondanza we cut into an ally. A freshly painted mural stretched along the back wall of a building. A gladiator stood larger than life in a heroic posture, an eagle standard raised triumphantly in the air. Below his feet, Felix was painting in embellished red lettering:

SPARTACUS VICTORIUS!

Two soldiers stumbled out from the back door of a tavern, squinting in the sunlight. We ducked beneath an outer staircase, sat down, leaned against the wall, and closed our eyes, pretending to be street urchins who had spent the night there. The soldiers lurched along, arms around each other's shoulders.

"'Spartacus victorious,'" one of them snorted.

"Not for long," the other laughed.

They pulled up their leather kilts and urinated at the feet of Spartacus for a long time.

"Ew!" Lucius whispered.

"Come tomorrow morning, Spartacus will get the surprise of his life."

"By tomorrow night, we'll be roasting him on a spit."

"Smart of the General to install our garrison near a salt mine, where Spartacus can't see it from the mountain."

When they turned the corner, we jumped up with excitement.

"Did you hear that?"

"They plan to attack tomorrow."

"We have to tell Spartacus."

I hesitated.

"You want to say goodbye to Simon," Felix said.

I smiled sheepishly.

"Go," Lucius said.

"We'll wait for you at the Necropolis," Felix added.

At the Scriptorium, I found Simon behind the counter, translating and copying text from one scroll to another. He was concentrating so intensely, he didn't hear me enter.

"We're leaving Pompeii," I said, in my best matter-of-fact voice.

He looked up from his work. "When?"

"Now. The Legion plans to attack tomorrow morning. We have to warn Spartacus."

"By which gate? What road will you take?"

"Porta Ercolano. A side street off Via Consolare leads past the Necropolis. I'm meeting Felix and Lucius at one of the mausoleums. We'll cut across the fields to a path that takes us to the foothills of Vesuvius."

We stood there looking at each other. I couldn't bear to go through another emotional goodbye. I was certain he couldn't, either.

"Good luck," was all he said.

"You, too."

I was glad we didn't hug. I would have burst into tears.

I found Felix and Lucius sitting in the shade of a two-story brick mausoleum with a peaked roof. Six marble busts were inset into niches that lined the top of the outer wall.

"We were starting to worry," Felix said.

A rhythmic pounding and clanking emerged in the distance. Then three blasts of a trumpet.

"Soldiers," Lucius whispered.

The pounding and clanking grew louder. A column of legionnaires marched down the road, their spears, shields, and swords clinking against their armor.

"In here," Felix whispered.

We opened the rusty gate and took several stone steps down into the sepulcher. The wall curved around in a semi-circle. Six marble pedestals were arranged in an arc, each holding a crystal urn in the shape of an animal.

A rabbit. A dog. A lion. A griffin. A wolf. A bull. A mural that wrapped around the wall illustrated a field of onions with Mount Vesuvius looming in the background. Casks of onions being loaded onto a ship. The ship on the high seas. Finally, the family of six, feasting on silver trays piled high with onions.

Through the entrance, we could see soldiers marching toward Porta Ercolano. Rows and rows of men, kicking up plumes of dust. The trumpet blasted two short, sharp toots. The men halted.

We crept into the shadowed recesses and crouched behind the pedestals. A third blast ricocheted off the monuments and echoed through the building. A one-word command was shouted. Then repeated along the column of men. Several dozen soldiers broke line and fanned out across the graveyard.

We huddled together, afraid to breathe. Had someone followed us? Or reported suspicious behavior? Were they searching for us?

A soldier stopped at the foot of a memorial statue of a patrician woman in a hooded robe and lifted his kilt to urinate. Lucius and I exchanged looks of disgust. Others chose their own monuments, mausoleums, and memorials for the same purpose.

The trumpet blasted five notes. The gate screeched open. Shouts, jeers, and jokes rang out as the soldiers hurried back into formation. A shadow appeared in the archway, the person's face obscured by darkness. We held our daggers ready.

The figure stepped inside and glanced around.

"Kalysta? . . . Felix? . . . Lucius?"

It was Simon, a bag slung across his shoulder.

"I've run away," he said. "I'm joining the Resistance."

11

Afternoon

We ran up the mountain to warn Spartacus the next legion was on its way.

To the work group of ten-to-fourteen-year-olds, he said, “I need you to create one hundred life-sized soldiers from sticks and vines. Supply them with real armor and weapons. Prop them up on posts lining the edge of the camp that faces northwest. They must be completed by nightfall.”

“Are we going to scare the Roman army with giant dolls?” I asked.

“Exactly.”

If this is Pater's plan, I thought, *all the rumors that he is a god have gone to his head.*

"Straw Man Olympics," Felix announced.

We worked in teams of three. Simon was chosen as official judge. He was considered unbiased and impartial because he favored no god of the Pantheon and none of our gods favored him. On our team, Felix managed the design concept and built the framework. Lucius gathered armor and weapons. I found a tunic, mantle, and sandals and stuffed them with hay.

"Let's name him Talos," Felix suggested.

"Who's Talos?" Lucius asked.

"Vulcan once created a colossal bronze robot-warrior, one hundred feet high, to protect Crete," Felix told us as we worked. "He named it Talos. Three times a day he marched around the perimeter of the island, keeping an eye out for approaching vessels. If an enemy or pirate ship threatened the port, Talos lobbed huge boulders onto the deck to sink it. He had a pet robot-dog named Laelaps."

Felix made a vine-and-stick Laelaps to accompany our Talos.

Everyone was instructed to pack our belongings and take down our tents. To pile extra wood on the line of fires that marked the main thoroughfare of our camp.

"Enough to burn through the night." Then Spartacus ordered us to, "Talk amongst yourselves."

People turned to one another asking, "What is the plan?"

We were told to become quieter and less talkative in turns, as if the camp were settling down for the night. Spartacus directed us to leave in clusters of about a hundred, following an ancient trail that led up the mountain. Two dozen men and women stayed behind, perched in trees. They spoke loudly in a variety of tones and voices, as if they were an entire army, drinking around their fires.

In this manner, three thousand people crept quietly away, leaving one hundred straw soldiers to guard an empty field.

Through the night, we wended our way up the slopes of Mount Vesuvius, scrambling over boulders that seemed to have been thrown down by ancient giants for the sole purpose of twisting ankles and slowing our progress. Wild grape vine wound around the trunks of every broom, beech, and locust tree. Everywhere, I heard the cries of children, complaining that they were cold, hungry, and tired. And the harsh whispers of mothers, stifling them with the threat of being kidnapped by a Roman Centurian.

Venus was still visible in pre-dawn sky when we stopped to rest. The ridge at the peak of Mount Vesuvius loomed above us, promising the last day of our upward trek would be the toughest. The crew of actors who had stayed behind ran into our midst.

Everyone asked, "What happened?"

"The Romans organized into battle formation and marched into the woods," one woman explained. "As they approached our encampment, they were met with an eerie silence. They suspected our warriors were concealed in the underbrush and behind the trees, waiting to ambush them. When they reached the edge of our camp, they came upon our soldier-dolls. Their commander shouted to these straw men, offering them a chance to surrender. He got no response from our intrepid scarecrows."

"His trumpeters blasted the call to charge. They advanced, their spears drawn. Thirty yards from our front line they stopped. They had noticed something wasn't right. The commander strode forward, shouting at our inanimate warriors. He thrust his sword into the belly of one of them. It didn't fall. The soldiers in front began to laugh. Soon, the joke passed through the ranks that their commander had been done in by a doll."

That was our second victory over the greatest army in human history.

"Sometimes the best way to win a battle," Spartacus grinned, "is to avoid it."

12

October-November

The summit of Mount Vesuvius was not so much a peak as a giant flat-bottomed bowl, a mile across, where we pitched our wandering village.

I stood gazing out over the towers of Pompeii to the topaz blue water of the Bay of Naples. Northwest along Via Appia lay Rome. To the northeast, vast white stretches of salt mines. At the back side of the mountain, a sheer cliff dropped into a lush river valley.

Spartacus assured us it would be a month or more before the Senate sent a third Legion. Meanwhile, life developed its own sort of normality.

At the Festival of Fortuna, we celebrated the end of the grape harvest with ten days of games and sports that Felix dubbed the Mini-Olympics. Throughout my childhood this had been a period not of joy and celebration, but of fear and anxiety. In Capua, it included ten days of gladiatorial games, once the most dreaded time of year for me. Spartacus had fought in the final combat of every festival, which meant Mater and I spent the days leading up to it frantically tossing offerings into the sacred fire and begging Dionysus to protect him.

Now that we were free, my friends encouraged me to compete. As it turned out, my years of running messages had paid off. I easily won three races and was awarded three laurel wreaths, which I offered in gratitude to the fires of Mercury. Each time I crossed a finish line first, I was greeted with hugs and cheers.

"You're as fast as Ladas," Felix said, invoking the legendary Spartan runner of Marathon.

Only to Simon did I admit the truth.

"Everyone is excited about my victories," I told him.

"And you're not?" he guessed.

"Is that bad? Shouldn't I be grateful for the ability to run fast?"

"Just because you're great at something doesn't mean you have to devote your life to it," he replied.

"What do you mean?"

"I'm good at translating Hebrew text into Greek and Latin. And vice versa. But I definitely do not want to devote my life to it. The Book Seller in Pompeii offered to rent or buy me from Batiatus so he could hire me full time. He promised to treat me as one of his sons. But the idea of spending the rest of my days sitting at a desk in a dusty scriptorium with a quill in my hand and ink stains on my tunic made me want to scream like a madman."

"Is that why you decided to run away?" I asked.

"Partly."

"But you love teaching. Why not return to Capua to tutor the children of Batiatus?"

"Those brats?" They don't care about literature. Or philosophy. They behave respectfully toward my pater and I because Batiatus commanded them to take their studies seriously. But I've seen how they treat the house slaves. The day before the breakout, I saw their daughter kick Lucius in the shins."

"Why?" Not that there could possibly have been any reason to hurt my dear friend.

"I think she was jealous that Lucilla—*Lucius*—is—*was*—prettier than—"

"*Shhh!*" I interrupted. "If Lucius hears you call him *pretty*, he will stab you in the neck."

"On my honor, I will henceforth eviscerate the p-word from my vocabulary," Simon assured me. "Anyway, I think that rich little twit was envious of Lucius. Of how much attention Domina paid her ancilla. My point is, I thought maybe here I could teach former slaves who appreciate the value of learning. Who might take an interest in how philosophy can guide them in their decisions as free individuals. And how literature can expand their perspective on life, history, and humanity."

By unstated agreement, Simon and I had not resumed my tutoring sessions. Life had a completely different structure and rhythm now. I was busy orienting newcomers and delivering messages. And he was busy gathering a following of students. I had loved being his private pupil. But the idea of being one among many didn't appeal to me. Besides, in this crowded village, always on the move, there was little time or space for something so selfish as private lessons.

The morning after the last day of games, Spartacus instructed our work group to gather the wild grape vines that twisted up and around every tree along the slopes.

"Only the longest, thickest, and greenest. When your arms are full, bring them back and head out for more."

"How many?" came the cry.

"Thousands."

"How long should they be?"

"As long as possible."

"Might as well ask Hercules to do it," Felix quipped.

"Who's Hercules?" Lucius asked.

"Hercules is a son of Jupiter," I explained. "He completed Twelve Labors, each one seemingly more impossible than the last. One of these tasks was to defeat the Hydra, a giant snake-monster with nine heads. It was easy to cut off the heads with his mighty sword. But each time he cut one off, two more heads grew in its place."

"Kinda like the Roman army," Lucius said.

"How so?" I asked.

"Every time we win a battle against a legion, they send twice as many soldiers to come after us."

"Hercules figured out that, if he used a flaming branch to cauterize the stump where each of the beast's heads was cut off, no more heads could grow back," I continued. Many times, I had seen Medicus cauterize Pater's wounds with a hot iron, to staunch the bleeding and prevent infection. "When Hercules had cut and cauterized eight of the Hydra's heads, he faced the ninth, which was immortal. First, he dipped the tips of his arrows in her poisonous blood. Then he buried the still-living head under a boulder."

"Hercules sounds like Donar," Lucius said.

"What's he like?" Felix asked.

"Donar is the eldest son of Mother Earth and the Sky God. He wears a golden belt that gives him superhuman strength and carries a giant hammer that he wields with magic gloves."

Before beginning our own Herculean labor, we gathered around a brassier.

"Hercules, son of Jupiter," Felix intoned, "Slayer of the Nemean Lion, the Stymphalian Birds, the nine-headed Hydra, and the Erymanthian Boar. Herder of the golden calf of Diana, the Cretan Bull, and the cattle of Geryon. Cleaner of the Augean Stables. Thief of the Mares of Diomedes, the girdle of the Amazonian Queen, and the apples of the Hesperides. Tamer of Cerberus, three-headed dog of the Underworld. We beseech you to grant us the endurance to gather thousands of strong, green, wild grape vines."

"In hope that you will aid us in our Herculean task," I added, "we will offer you our first vine."

Thus began the Vine-Gathering Olympics.

Day after day, we tromped through the woods in search of the longest, greenest, and strongest vines. Lucius climbed as high as he could to cut them with his dagger. Felix and I stood at the base, pulling on them as he shimmied down. We dragged back armfuls of vines and piled them up at one end of the camp. Each night, when we presented Spartacus with our harvest, he made only one comment.

"More."

"What are we going to do with them?" we asked one another.

"Maybe we'll lasso the Roman squadrons," Lucius suggested, "like wrangling wild horses."

"Or challenge them to a thousand rounds of tug-of-war," I offered.

"Or swing from tree to tree and pounce on their heads from above," Felix mused.

Each morning was frostier than the last. Wasps landed on our mid-day meals, desperate to collect the last sweetness of the year. The fruit of the Mastic trees turned from orange to red to purple. We scraped off wads of sap with our daggers and chewed it like gum, releasing the peppermint-black-pepper-anise flavor that delighted our senses and caused us to salivate like dogs.

Spartacus scrutinized our mountain of vines.

"Now weave them into ropes."

"How thick?"

"Strong enough to hold the weight of a gladiator."

"How many?"

"Five hundred ropes of at least five hundred feet in length. If the vines aren't long enough, tie them together. Begin by braiding three sets of three vines. Then braid those nine vines into a single rope."

"Vine Olympics," Felix announced. "Weaving event."

Standing around a brazier, each of us braided a lock of our own hair, cut it with our daggers, and tossed it into the flames.

"Athena, daughter of Jupiter, goddess of weavers, wisdom, and sailors," I began. "Please help us to braid thousands of vines into five-hundred sturdy ropes of at least five-hundred feet long. I offer you this braided lock of my hair, in hope that you will give my hands the strength and dexterity to complete this Herculean task."

For weeks, we sat on the ground, weaving vines into ropes. We asked the younger children to bring us food, that we might grab bites without losing our pattern. Late at night, women came out of their tents demanding that we stop long enough to rest.

The Eagle star rose in the sky. We could see our breath in the frosty night air. The Romans were that much closer to freezing or starving us out of our sanctuary at the crest of the mountain. I thanked Athena for giving me the will to continue weaving until my hands bled.

"Wake up." Lucius shook my shoulder.

"What?" I asked grumpily, swatting his hands away.

"I need your help."

I followed sleepily as he wove erratically around and between hundreds of tents.

"Here," he pronounced, stamping the dirt.

I spun in a slow circle. "Is this the center of the crater?"

"Exactly."

"What are we doing?"

"This." He handed me a rectangular sheet of thin, soft lead.

"A curse tablet?"

He nodded. I read the engraving in the ambient light of the stars.

I call upon and beseech

the 3 Furies of Vengeance

to inflict upon

DOMINA BATIATUS

of Capua

a terrible, painful, and disfiguring

skin disease

from which she will find no relief

Until the day she frees every slave and

gladiator in the House of Batiatus

In the name of Revenge for

her ~~former ancilla~~

LUCIUS OF THE ZARUBINTZY

On the back, Lucius had scratched a stick figure of Domina, bound in twine from head to toe.

"Did I tell you she 'gave' me a name?" Lucius asked bitterly. "She called me Kitty."

He spat on the tablet, rolled the soft metal like a papyrus scroll, and pressed two nails through it. Next, he wound a long strand of dark hair around the scroll and tied it off.

"Domina's hair." Lucius flashed a grin full of vengeful glee. "I ripped it from her head as I was stabbing her."

"You kept it all this time?"

"I knew even then exactly what I would use it for."

Lucius fell to his knees and began to dig.

Still sleepy, I stood with my eyes closed. I wasn't sure how I felt about curse tablets. Making an offering to a god to pray for their help was one thing. But calling down a curse upon another person?

Then I thought of all Lucius had suffered. The death of his pater at the hands of a hostile tribe. His mater, sold into slavery, the gods knew where. His village, looted, ransacked, and burned to the ground. The humiliation of being a boy forced to dress as an ancilla.

I could not imagine myself creating a curse tablet. But I had never suffered as Lucius had.

"That's deep enough." Lucius stood up and stretched his back with satisfaction. He placed the curse tablet in the ground, buried it and stamped on the dirt. Then he did a weird dance, a sort of jig, chanting coarse, ominous words in his native tongue.

13

December

"They're coming!"

"The Romans are marching up the mountain!"

"They will push us off the cliff!"

The camp was in an uproar.

Spartacus stepped calmly from his tent. Everyone grew silent.

"The time has come," he announced.

There was not a man, woman, or child among us who did not have complete faith that he would lead us safely to freedom.

Our warriors secured the five hundred vine-ropes to five hundred trees that grew close to the cliff at the back of the mountain. I grabbed a rope and, pressing my toes against the rock face, walked backward while easing my way down, hand under hand under hand. Others who had gathered the vines and woven the ropes followed my lead. Children were encouraged to go next. When they reached the ground, we congratulated and hugged them. Then women with babies strapped to their backs or toddlers clinging to their shoulders. Most of the remaining adults followed.

Goats, sheep, mules, and dogs were harnessed and lowered. Then baskets of supplies, tools, weapons, cats, tents, chickens, and food.

The warriors rappelled down, pushing their powerful legs against the wall as they swung out and walked their hands down before swinging back to propel themselves out and down again. Finally, Spartacus rappelled down in a few spectacular swoops.

Three thousand people chanted, "Spar-ta-KUS! Spar-ta-KUS!"

The din of a thousand spears banging against shields clattered down from the cliff, drowning them out. I craned my neck to look up. The toes of hundreds of pairs of sandals peeked over the edge. The Romans had reached the summit and were peering down in wonderment at their prey. A mass of former slaves, standing out of reach of the long arm of Rome.

"To the ropes!" the General commanded.

I sucked in my breath. Why hadn't Spartacus anticipated that they would use our ropes to pursue us?

But none of the soldiers seemed eager to obey. Equipped with swords, spears, shields, helmets, armor, and heavy packs, these legionnaires were not trained or clad for scaling down cliffs. Or for plunging, feet first, into a sea of people who hated them.

"Down!" the General barked.

The soldiers didn't budge.

"Climb down!"

None obeyed.

"Now! Or you will be beaten for desertion."

That got their attention. But no one moved.

We taunted them with shouts and jeers.

"Come and get us!"

"Afraid of a few thousand slaves?"

"Even a child can do it!"

"Starting with you!" the general screamed. He pummeled the soldier next to him with the butt of his sword until the man grabbed a vine and stepped backward over the edge to evade his blows. Several others grabbed hold of the vines and walked backward over the edge.

The smell of smoke arose from behind me. Dozens of women held sticks to a freshly lit fire and touched them to the vines. The fire shot upward. The flaming vines swayed under the weight of the legionnaires. Giant green snakes danced on the tips of their tails, their impossibly long bodies stretched upward, their red tongues lashing at the ankles of our enemies.

A wave of shouts erupted from the soldiers. They turned and fled back down the front of the mountain. Their commander hesitated only moments before following.

A faint cry emanated from halfway up the cliff. I thought it might be a kid goat that hadn't been lowered all the way down. Then I heard a child screaming.

"Mommy!"

A toddler sat on a narrow ledge, a pet rabbit clutched to her chest. I grabbed a rope that hadn't caught fire and pulled myself up. The smoke filled my nostrils and stung my eyes. Seeing me, the girl stood on wobbly legs. I held the rope with my right hand and stretched out my left arm as far as I could. Only the tips of my fingers reached her ankles.

The girl leaned forward then lost her balance and fell. I gasped as I grabbed the back of her nappy. With one arm, I hugged her to my chest. She wrapped her chubby little arms around my neck, the rabbit squished between us.

"What's your name?" I asked.

"Gemma."

"Hang on tight, Gemma."

I clambered down, hand-under-hand, my eyes squeezed shut against the smoke. My feet hadn't touched the ground when the girl cried, "Mama!" reaching out to her mater, who took her from my arms.

I fell to the ground. My lungs felt as if I had inhaled shards of glass. Laying on my back, I stared at the charred stripes of ash running vertically up the cliff. My left arm, from wrist to shoulder, burned with pain. Antigone was charcoal-gray.

Mater spread unguent over my burnt flesh and rubbed it into Antigone's skin. The snake's body pulsed as if stricken with seizures. A layer of charred skin separated from her head then pealed itself along the length of her body to her tail. She shimmied out of it, leaving a translucent, wheat-colored husk on the ground beside me. She looked perky and vivacious in a fresh layer of iridescent green skin.

Hesperos, the Herdsman's Star, appeared in the western sky. The Goat Horn constellation rose, marking the Winter Solstice. A goat was sacrificed to Prometheus. Spartacus placed its bones and hooves, wrapped in its hide, on the fire with words of gratitude. Mater threw handfuls of spices and incense into the flames, thanking Prometheus for harnessing the fire that saved us from the Romans. The aroma of peppermint burst forth in green sparks, followed by cinnamon in a flower of orange bursts, and Frankincense in explosions of purple.

I tossed the dry, crunchy shell of Antigone's molted skin into the flames. It crackled and shriveled to ash. A snake-like lick of green flame rose up from the smoke and floated into the heavens.

"To Prometheus, Giver of Fire," I intoned. "Thank you for giving me the courage to rescue Gemma. And for saving her bunny from being crushed to death. And protecting Antigone and me from being burned worse than we were."

More goats were butchered, roasted on spits, and basted in a sauce of pepper, wild onion, honey, wine, and olive oil. Dessert was honey custard topped with roasted pine nuts, pistachios, and dried pears.

I sat around a fire with Felix, Lucius, and Simon. Antigone's skin sparkled in the flickering light.

"Who's Prometheus?" Lucius asked.

"Prometheus is a Titan," I began. "He created humans by molding us from clay and river water. Then animating us with the breath of life. He taught us the skills that separate us from animals. Language. Art. Music. Farming. Architecture. Metallurgy. Writing."

I paused, afraid of dominating the conversation.

"Keep going," Lucius urged.

"Jupiter forbade the gods from sharing with humans the secret to fire," I continued. "But Prometheus took pity on us, seeing our ancient ancestors shiver in their caves during winter. Gnashing their teeth on raw meat. Living a meager existence without metal tools. He stole a flaming fennel branch from Mount Olympus and carried it down to earth. He taught humans how to make fire using flint and steel. How to roast meat. To heat our homes. To bake bread. To smelt metals."

"Jupiter, seeing how fire empowered humans, was enraged. When he learned Prometheus was the source of our newfound skills, Jupiter determined to punish him. Because Prometheus is immortal and cannot be killed, Jupiter chained him to a rock that hung out from a cliff in the Caucus Mountains. Every day, a golden eagle was sent to peck out Prometheus's liver. Each night, his liver grew back. But the next day, the eagle returned to continue inflicting his cruel sentence."

"Is Prometheus still chained to the rock?" Lucius wondered.

"Hercules freed him." I explained. "Thirty thousand years later."

"Why is Jupiter so mean?" Lucius asked.

"I don't know." I had never before heard a person criticize a god. "I guess because he's the King of the Gods and can do whatever he wants."

"He sounds selfish," Lucius persisted.

"He spends most of his time cheating on his wife. Then trying to hide the evidence by killing his own children." I thought for a moment. "Or trying to prevent humans from gaining too much power over our own destinies."

Lucius smirked.

"Okay, sure," I laughed. "Jupiter is selfish."

"Kind of like the Romans," he observed. "They hate for anyone who isn't Roman to thrive or succeed."

"Is the king of your gods any better?" I asked.

"Odin, our Sky Father, loves mortals. He sits on a golden throne with two wolves by his side. On his shoulders sit two ravens, named Thought and Memory. Every day they fly over the earth and at night report back to him on what humans have been up to."

"Sounds like a nice guy," I said, a little defensively. But the more I thought about it, I could see Lucius's point. No wonder Jupiter was the favorite god of the Romans.

Lucius continued, "Odin once went down to the Well of Wisdom and begged Mimir the Wise for a draught of sacred water. Mimir agreed only if Odin was willing to sacrifice one of his eyes to gain this wisdom."

"I'm not sure Jupiter has much to offer in the way of wisdom," I admitted. "Usually, he does really foolish things. Then comes up with ridiculous ways of trying to hide his mistakes from his wife."

"Odin sacrificed his own eye to make our lives better," Lucius went on. "He shared his newfound wisdom with his beloved humans. Later, he chose to pay the price of suffering a constant, mysterious pain for the rest of his days, in exchange for learning the mysteries of the runes."

"Okay, I see your point," I admitted. "Jupiter is a jerk. And he isn't very smart. I've never liked him anyway. I've never once visited his temple or made an offering to him." I turned to Simon. "You have only one god. Is he selfish or self-sacrificing? Mean or nice? Foolish or wise?"

"He's no fool," Simon answered thoughtfully. "He can be mean when he's angry with the Jews for disobeying him. I wouldn't say he's selfish. But he is exacting. He expects us to obey every commandment to the letter."

"Our gods don't have rules or laws," Felix mused. "The only thing they expect is that we make offerings to assure them we haven't forgotten them. That they are always in our thoughts."

"The Jewish laws are for the same purpose," Simon reflected. "To demonstrate to God that he is always in our thoughts. And that we are forever grateful to Him for blessing us with wine and bread and the laws of Moses. And a thousand other things."

"But is your god *nice*?" I persisted. "Does he do things to help people?"

"He parted the Red Sea to help the Jews escape slavery in Egypt. Then, as Pharoah's army was pursuing them, he caused the sea to come crashing down and drown them."

"We could use a god like that to drown the Roman army," Felix said.

Later, Simon and I sat side by side, apart from the others.

"You made a heroic choice today," he said.

"Gemma? I didn't really think about it. I heard her crying. Then I saw her. I had to try."

"You didn't *have* to. You *chose* to."

"I guess."

"You are the kind of person who does not stand idly by while others are suffering," he said with special emphasis.

I thought of the countless afternoons when I had watched the slave auction and done nothing to stop it.

"In the ludus that night, you took *all* the butcher knives."

"I saw them and decided to put them in my bag. Just in case."

"*Decided* to. . .. In *case* . . . what?"

"In case someone needed them."

"At the back of your mind, you were thinking more knives could mean more escaped gladiators."

"True," I admitted.

"You gave Lucius your dagger, at the risk of being caught." He paused. "And you ran back to invite me to escape with you," he added, more quietly.

"That was because I couldn't bear the thought of never seeing you again!" I blurted out.

Even as I was saying it, I regretted it. Simon was suddenly quiet. My statement hovered between us like a smoldering gryphon. I wanted to take my words back. To tell him I didn't really mean what I'd said. But that would have made it worse by making a big deal about it.

I waited for him to speak. To respond. To say *anything*. I hoped most of all that he would change the subject. Pretend he hadn't heard me.

He stared into the fire as if he'd forgotten I was there. Then he stood up. "I have to go."

I assumed he had stepped into the woods to pee and would return shortly. But he didn't.

I sat with my elbows on my knees, chin in my hands, staring into the fire. I had always felt comfortable with Simon. He had always encouraged me to share my thoughts and ideas with him. *But not my feelings.*

I felt like Pandora.

After Prometheus taught the secret of fire to humans, Jupiter resented that it empowered mortals to be more like gods. He wanted us to remain weak and helpless. To make life more difficult, Jupiter commanded Vulcan to create an artificial woman, so lifelike no one would suspect she was a robot. He named her Pandora and gave her a jar filled with thousands upon thousands of invisible creatures that could inflict every possible pain, suffering, and misery. He sent her down to earth to mingle with people. When she opened the jar, every type of plague, horror, and tragedy was unleashed upon humanity.

Revealing to Simon how I felt about him that night months ago in Capua felt like opening Pandora's jar. But instead of a jar, I had opened my heart. Instead of a plague, what poured out was a flood of feelings.

It might as well have been a plague. I felt certain I had ruined our friendship. It didn't help that, while I was still twelve, he was now fourteen. Maybe, like Tavia, he had outgrown my friendship.

After that night, I avoided Simon. Avoided talking to him. Avoided crossing paths with him. Avoided sitting next to him around the fire. And there was no way I would ever again risk making eye contact with him.

This proved to be easy. It was obvious he was trying as hard to avoid me as I was to avoid him.

Part III

ROMAN YEAR 438

14

Winter

Our wandering village had grown to fifty thousand.

On January 1, we celebrated the Festival of Janus, god of doorways, openings, arches, beginnings, and transitions. People exchanged gifts of dried fruit, nuts, and olives, which we tossed into the fire, hoping for good omens of the coming year. Spartacus sacrificed a goat to thank Janus for blessing our transition to a new era of Freedom.

Simon and I settled into the new form our friendship had taken. In a group, it was easy to avoid talking to each other one-on-one. We exchanged pleasantries. Were cordial. Avoided meaningful conversation. Avoided being alone together.

Meanwhile, Simon had attracted two dozen followers. He and his students strolled through the camp as well as the surrounding fields and woods, discussing philosophical ideas about nature and human behavior. For lessons in reading and writing Latin and Greek, they sat in a broad circle under a tree or open-air tent. As with me, he required each student to stand while reciting the *Fables* of Aesop or passages from Homer's *Iliad* or *Odyssey*. I frequently saw him surrounded by a cluster of students who drank in his every word. They addressed him as *Grammaticus* and revered him as the young wise man I knew him to be.

One day I was about to enter Pater's command tent when I literally bumped into Simon, who was just leaving.

"Oh!" we both said.

"What are you doing here?" I asked.

"I was meeting . . . with Spartacus."

Of course. What else would he be doing in Spartacus' tent?

"Why?" I persisted. "What about?"

"Nothing, really."

"About *me*?"

"No," he replied evenly.

Of course not. What reason would Simon have to talk about me to my Pater?

"We were discussing . . . politics."

"Politics?"

"Anyway, I need to get going. My students are waiting for me to give a lesson on the differences between the Greek and Latin alphabets."

Inside, Pater sat at his strategy table, looking intently at an open scroll. As far as I knew, he didn't have the skills to read an actual scroll. Growing up as a shepherd, he had had no formal education. As a gladiator and slave, he had been forbidden tutoring lessons. Of course, like many slaves, he could write his name and jot down and decipher short written messages. But I had never known him to sit down and read a scroll.

"What's that?" I asked.

"This?" He ruffled the top edge of the papyrus. "It's a speech. From the Senate."

"I . . . didn't know you liked reading speeches."

My real question hovered between us like a nervous griffin: *Since when have you learned to read the extended, formal style of writing used in Senatorial speeches?*

"I need to understand how Senators think," he explained. "How they go about their business. How decisions are made in the Forum. It will help me to strategize our way out of this." He pointed to the middle of the page and cleared his throat. "*Malo peric . . . ulosam libertatem . . . quam quietam . . . servitutem."*

He sounded out each syllable, like a child learning to recognize clusters of letters as individual words.

"Malo periculosam libertatem quam quietam servitutem," he repeated with confidence.

I would rather enjoy dangerous freedom than peaceful enslavement.

He grinned like a schoolboy, proud of himself for making it through an entire sentence without stumbling.

Of course! Simon was teaching Spartacus to read. But instead of bothering with *Aesop's Fables,* Pater had dived right into political speeches. I now understood why Simon had been evasive about what he'd been doing in the Command Tent. Spartacus didn't want word to get out that he was being tutored to read. It somewhat diminished his reputation as a demi-god.

"What does it mean?" I asked.

"It's from a speech given by a former Consul. When he said it, he didn't mean actual *slavery.* It turns out Senators use the word 'slavery' to describe situations where they feel that other politicians have gotten the better of them. When a Senator they oppose wins an election or gets his way in passing a law, those who oppose him refer to themselves as being 'enslaved' by their opponent."

Spartacus asked Felix to paint:

PERICULOSAM LIBERTATEM

on the entrance to his Command Tent.

The phrase quickly grew popular. Many of the warriors had it tattooed on their forearms or painted on the inside of their shields. It became their battle cry.

After that, I frequently crossed paths with Simon outside Pater's tent. Sometimes in the afternoons I found the two of them intently focused on strategy board games, such as Mercenaries, Little Thieves, and Twelve Writings.

15

Spring

March was dedicated to celebrations in honor of Mars, God of War.

On the first, a parade to welcome the start of the military season processed through the center of camp. Warriors in full armor marched in formation, banging their spears and sword hilts against their shields. They periodically stopped to break into crazy antics, leaping, skipping, and twirling. Because wolves are the favorite animal of Mars, the dogs were encouraged to join in. They mimicked the erratic movements of the soldiers, jumping and barking with excitement. The day culminated in a reenactment of the legendary fight between Mars and a Dragon.

My thirteenth birthday arrived in mid-March. Mater gave me a bronze hand mirror, with the back molded in the image of Prometheus. I had occasionally seen myself in a mirror, when in the marketplace I had picked one up, pretending to consider buying it. But what I now saw in the obsidian reflection gave me an earie feeling, as if I were looking at my own ghost.

"That's you," I said to the circular image gazing back at me. "I mean, that's *me*."

Antigone was transfixed, sending herself into a trance by staring into her own eyes.

"Mirrors aren't good for snakes," I told her.

She lost interest and tapped the underside of my chin with the top of her head.

In Capua, wealthy women spent fortunes on expensive hand mirrors. Lucius had seen Domina gaze into her mirror for hours, as if she expected it to reveal the secret to happiness. But I didn't understand the fascination. The mirror did not help me to answer the important questions. It did not provide insight that led me to deeper self-knowledge. It did not reveal my strengths of character. It did not guide me in making wise decisions. It seemed more like a performer's trick. A magician's slight-of-hand or juggler's gambit or fire-swallower's flourish. Mildly entertaining. Otherwise, not worth dwelling upon.

"Maybe mirrors aren't good for girls, either," I whispered.

"Have you decided on a tattoo?" my parents asked.

In our tribe, girls at thirteen are allowed to choose their first tattoo.

"Yes," I replied. "An owl."

"You feel a strong affinity with Athena," Mater nodded.

For months, I had been thinking about what tattoo I wanted. Which god would I most like to emulate? What permanent symbol should I choose to define my identity? Or to guide me in striving to become the best possible version of myself?

I still felt that I didn't entirely know myself. And I hadn't found my calling in life. But I sensed I was on the right path. That I would discover my true self along the way. Simon's ideal of striving for a good life through self-knowledge and wise decisions had stuck with me. I wondered how I might translate these ideas into a tattoo.

That got me thinking about Athena.

"Athena is a daughter of Jupiter," Mater told me. "When she was born, he didn't want her, so he tossed her into his mouth and swallowed her. Immediately after, he complained to his friend Vulcan that he had a terrible headache. Vulcan swung his axe and split Jupiter's head open. Out of her father's head popped Athena, fully grown and clad in the armor of a warrior."

Unlike many gods, Athena was a friend to mortals. She helped Hercules in several of his Twelve Labors. She helped Bellerophon tame Pegasus. She helped Jason to seize the Golden Fleece from the Dragon. She helped Perseus to cut off the head of Medusa, the snake-haired monster whose gaze turned men to stone. She helped Telemachus to search for his pater Odysseus, who had not returned after the Trojan War. And she helped Odysseus to find his way home after ten years of wandering at sea.

Athena was a warrior, goddess of weavers, and protector of sailors. But she was also *smart.* Her owl symbolized her *metis*—cleverness, intelligence, and wisdom.

"Athena is a fine choice," my parents agreed.

I ran to find Boudica, who drew a sketch of Athena's owl with big, friendly eyes. Over the following days, she made ink from crushed berries, stones, and shells, mixed with watered-down clay, which she needled below the surface of the skin on my back, one painful pinprick at a time.

One afternoon I noticed Simon's students standing in a field, holding a blanket by the edges. As I approached, I saw among them Vitalio, Thalus, Anthusa, Ursula, and Damalis. Simon lay in the center of the blanket, looking vulnerable and uncertain.

"One . . . Two . . . Three . . ." they called out. Then, shouting, "Huzzah!" they simultaneously raised their arms, stretching the blanket taught.

Simon was propelled into the air, his arms and legs flailing helplessly.

Cheering, "Gratitude!" they lowered their arms to catch him in the cradle of the blanket.

Again, shouting, "Huzzah!" they raised their arms, propelling him even higher. Again, cheering, "Gratitude!" they lowered their arms, allowing the blanket to catch him.

"Why are you tormenting your *Grammaticus*?" I asked Vitalio.

"We're honoring him," he assured me. "We toss him as high as we can, to symbolize the height of our respect for him. When we catch him, we demonstrate that he can trust in our devotion to his teachings."

I wasn't so sure Simon was enjoying the honor. Each time he began his descent, I worried the exhausted arms of his students would fail him, that they would drop the blanket and he would land painfully on the hard ground.

"Want to take an edge?" Ursula offered. "The more of us there are, the more honor we bestow upon him."

And the less likely he is to fall to his death, I thought.

Vitalio and Ursula made room for me to grab an edge of the blanket.

"One . . . Two . . . Three . . . Huzzah!" I shouted with the others, lifting my arms as high as I could.

For a fleeting moment, as Simon was hurdled into the air, he locked eyes with me. When he landed, he flashed a grin.

I wondered if I had overreacted to his non-reaction to the feelings I had blurted out that night by the fire three months earlier. It was more that I had felt embarrassed by my emotional outburst. I wondered if I were the one avoiding him, more than he was avoiding me. Besides, now that I was thirteen and he was still fourteen, I felt I had "caught up" with him. Finally, we were both teens. Maybe our friendship wasn't as broken as I thought.

I had vowed that, if it were to be repaired, he would have to make the first gesture. Was his fleeting grin as he landed on the blanket that gesture?

The next general to be sent after us was Varinius. His Legion marched aimlessly along their well-built roads, never sure where we might pop up next. They were certain they could defeat us—if only they could find us!

In their first skirmish, Spartacus captured Varinius's war horse. After that, he rode the liberated steed into every battle. The people's faith in him grew stronger. Rumors spread that he was the son of Athena, Goddess of War.

16

Summer

On the Summer Solstice we celebrated Fortuna, goddess of chance, luck, fortune, fate, and destiny. The Bakers made honey cakes shaped like wheels, to symbolize the Wheel of Fortune.

In mid-July we held sporting competitions, games, and theatrical performances in honor of Apollo. Simon organized his students to recite the complete epics of Homer's *Iliad* and *Odyssey* in turns, continuing non-stop for three days and three nights.

He lent the Sappho scroll to Lucius, who recruited a dozen boys and girls to perform them as choral songs with coordinated dances and musical accompaniment from a lyre.

The play was a comedy, performed on an outdoor stage, about a slave who outwits his Dominus. Vitalio played the foolish Dominus. Felix played the clever slave. Their best lines were received with peals of laughter. It was refreshing to devote time to mirth, after all the struggles and hardships we had endured.

That night at the bonfire I noticed Felix and Vitalio holding hands. I felt a pang of envy, wondering if Simon and I would ever hold hands around the fire. There was no point in pretending to myself that I didn't mind how distant we had become over the past six months. Now that I was thirteen and he was fourteen, I saw no reason why he wouldn't think of me *in that way*. I was no longer a kid. I had a tattoo covering my back to prove it.

I had observed—more like scrutinized—Simon's interactions with his students—during their lessons as well as times of leisure—and found no evidence that he favored any one of them. Once, I had noticed from a distance that he was speaking in meaningful concentration with someone, their heads tilted toward one another, and instantly felt a bloom of passionate jealousy erupt in my chest.

But, on getting closer, I saw that it was Spartacus with whom he spoke. Not some eager, sweet-faced budding scholar, as I had imagined. I stood watching their backs from a distance, not wanting to interrupt but dying to know what important matter they were discussing. Then Spartacus set his arm loosely across Simon's shoulder, as a father to a favorite son. I could hardly believe it. This is the manner in which a father might embrace a young man of whom he approves as a future match for his daughter.

I knew that my pater would never engage in such a negotiation over my future, as tribal peoples leave it to their youths to choose our own mates based on natural attraction and affinity. But it left me with a strong feeling that the thought has crossed his mind. And that, were Simon and I to one day choose each other, he would be pleased to see me united with a young man for whom he clearly held both respect and fatherly affection.

I could no longer fool myself with the brittle sheen of needless resentment I had built up toward Simon. For what? Because I was embarrassed by something I had said, after which he had retired to his tent without responding or bidding me goodnight? Maybe he genuinely hadn't heard me, when I blurted out, "I was afraid I would never see you again!" I had certainly known him to be so lost in thought that he didn't hear others speaking to him. And my perception that I had shouted my feelings to him could have been wrong. For all I knew, I may have shamefacedly mumbled it under my breath.

And why pretend to myself that I had not had a girlish crush on him since we were nine and eleven? I could see clearly now that, when I was eleven and he was thirteen, he must have regarded me as dangerously young. What boy would want to cross the great Spartacus by messing with his little girl, his only daughter?

I was in love with Simon. I felt certain he must be in love with me. Even if he hadn't quite allowed himself to admit it to himself yet. I couldn't imagine either of us being with anyone else. Could he be waiting—ever so patiently—for me to let him know I was now old enough for him?

Still, I couldn't be certain. And to raise the question directly would be to risk rejection. Everyone knows that teen boys and young men expect to dabble in all manner of romantic encounters before they married. And, though my Thracian parents had married at thirteen and fourteen, Romans preferred to save their sons until they were at least twenty-one, before marrying them off to girls of fourteen to sixteen. And who knew how the Jews regarded these matters?

For the August Festival of Diana, Lucius led a group of girls and boys in a ritual of washing our hair in a river to honor the goddess of wilderness.

A few days later, Spartacus oversaw the Festival of Portunas, god of keys, leading all who cared to join him in throwing thousands of shackle keys into the river.

Soon after was the Festival of Vinalia Rustica, for which we plucked handfuls of unripe grapes and threw them into the fire to pray for successful ripening of the harvest.

Crowded into this full schedule was the Festival of Vulcanalia. We caught tiny fish with shimmering rainbow scales and tossed them into the fire, beseeching Vulcan to protect the ripening crops from blight, fire, draught, and flooding.

Despite these celebrations, a dark undercurrent of doubt and dissent flowed through our community. Our slave revolt was suffering an identity crisis. So far, our army had engaged with six different Roman legions. Always on our terms. Always by surprise. By ambush.

We had defeated the army of Consul Cn. Cornelius Lentulus Coldianus. We had been victorious over the army of Consuls L. Gellius and Q. Arrius. In every battle we had roundly defeated our opponents. Again and again,

Roman soldiers ran in terror from our "barbarian" warriors. One after another general returned to Rome with his tail between his legs, ashamed to have been defeated by a rag-tag band of runaways they considered to be sub-human.

But what was our ultimate goal? Where would it all end? For the first time, Spartacus and Crixus openly disagreed. Crixus, buoyed by our victories, was for continuing the fight. He and many others wanted to keep up the revenge attacks and pillaging on villas of the wealthy.

Spartacus held a meeting about the long-term goal of our Rebellion.

"In the end, we can't win this war," he announced.

"Why not?" Crixus asked. "Again and again, we have humiliated the Romans."

"They will win in the end," Spartacus assured us. "We are fifty-thousand. Only twenty thousand of us are warriors. The vast Roman Republic has an endless supply of men to draft into their forces. Resources to create an endless supply of weapons. An endless supply of grain to keep them marching. We have used the elements of surprise, of hide-and-seek, of ambush, successfully. So far. If, and when, we face them head on in a traditional battle, they will win."

"What else can we do?" the people asked. "Give up?"

"Many of us have a homeland we still remember, or that our parents remember," Spartacus reminded them. "Clanfolk and tribes living across the Alpine Mountains. Westward into Gaul. East along the Danube River. North, on the banks of the Rhine River. We cannot remain free in Italy. But we can go home."

"The fierce tribes north of the Danube have been fighting off Roman invasion for generations," Lucius told me.

"My people in Gaul are fighting the Romans even now," Boudica commented, "defending our lands against further conquest."

Spartacus nodded. "We must return to our homelands, whether already conquered or still unconquered. We must join the fight for our native territories. If we remain in Italy, we may win another six battles. Another ten battles. Another twenty. But we will still have nowhere to settle."

"Freedom without a home is an endless struggle," Mater told me later.

"Pater says freedom is always a struggle," I reminded her.

"Some kinds of freedom are more fragile than others," she noted.

For weeks, there were arguments. Should we head north to the Alps? Or keep fighting the Romans? Most were happy to continue alternately fighting and evading the legions. Their main joy in life had become revenge. They wanted only to kill those who had made them suffer so greatly.

"Revenge should not be an end in itself," Spartacus reminded us. "Freedom is but one goal. We have to find a place to settle. To make a *home.* We mustn't be like the dog who barked at his own shadow."

"Who is the dog that barked at its shadow?" Lucius asked around the fire that night.

"It's one of Aesop's Fables," I began. "A dog kills a stag and carries in his mouth a haunch of meat to take back to his family. On the way home, he crosses a bridge over a still stream. Seeing his own reflection in the water, he thinks it's another dog, carrying an even bigger piece of meat than the one in his own jaws. To scare the illusory dog and seize its meat, he barks at his own reflection. When he opens his mouth to bark, his meat falls into the water and drifts away. He is left with nothing."

"What does it mean?" Feilx asked.

"I have no idea," I admitted.

"Revenge in itself cannot be the path to a good life," Simon explained.

"So is revenge the meat?" Felix persisted. "And a good life is the dog's shadow?"

"The real meat is *freedom,* which the dog clutches in his mouth," Simon explained. "The *reflection* of the meat is *revenge*—an *illusion* of freedom. The dog sacrifices his *freedom* (symbolized by the meat) in an effort to grasp at *revenge* (the illusory meat)."

"What's wrong with revenge?" Lucius asked.

"The Stoics would say, if revenge is your only motivation for the decisions you make, you're not living your best life," Simon replied.

A vote was held. Ten thousand opted to follow Crixus, heading to Rome, hellbent on revenge.

Felix had a long talk with his pater, which he told me about later. He explained to Crixus that he wanted to devote his life to art—not revenge. To creating—not killing. And that he did not want to leave Vitalio.

"You're just like your mater," Crixus told him.

"You've never really told me about her."

"She came from a clan of Mauritanian weavers. She was sold to Batiatus as a young woman and put to work on their loom. Her blankets were beautiful. She made that Tanit pendant when she was pregnant with you."

"How am I like her?"

"Like you, she hated violence. She refused to be told when my gladiatorial combats were scheduled. Or if I had won or lost. 'If I never see you again,' she used to say, 'I'll know you have retired to the sands.'"

"As for me, violence is all I've ever known," Crixus continued. "When I was a boy in Lucitania, I remember only fear of Roman attacks on our village. I was eight when my parents fought and died resisting the army of Licinius Crassus. I was sold into slavery as a prisoner of war and forced to work in the silver mines. Six years later I was sold to Batiatus. I soon discovered I'm good at killing people. I was winning gladiatorial combats by the age of sixteen. Now I can't imagine doing anything *but* fight. Violence is the only thing I've ever known."

"But it's not too late," Felix pleaded. "You're free now. You can do whatever you want."

"I must fight Rome so that you can devote your life to art and friendship," Crixus replied.

"Vitalio is more than a friend to me," Felix reminded him.

"Yes, I know. I will fight Rome so that you may follow your heart," his pater concluded.

Felix cried, knowing he may never again see his pater. I wondered if I would one day have to choose between following my parents and following my own path.

I expected Lucius, as a warrior and among the bitterest of former slaves, to follow Crixus. But I learned that he was determined to reunite with his clan and had chosen to continue north with Spartacus.

Spartacus warned Crixus and his followers again and again, "We do not have the military machinery to seize a city with defensive walls thirteen feet thick."

"Then we will die trying!" Crixus assured him.

The rest of us chose to follow Spartacus to the Alps.

17

Autumn

For months we trekked north along the Apennine Mountain range that forms the spine of the Italian peninsula. We traveled at night, through rocky, mountainous terrain and thick forests. Six hundred miles. The further north we went, the more escaped slaves joined us.

Now sixty-thousand strong, we came down from the mountains and crossed the Po River to enter the province of Cisalpine Gaul. This region had once been Roman. Then it was invaded by Celts. Recently it had been reconquered by Rome.

Meanwhile, the Roman army was preoccupied with tracing the path of attacks and raids led by Crixus as his followers progressed toward Rome. In September, remnants of the splinter army of Crixus straggled back from a horrific defeat by the army of Propraetor Q. Arrius. Felix's pater was not among them. We were told Crixus had died bravely on the battlefield.

Only when I learned this did it strike me that, since the breakout, I had never once worried that my Pater might die in battle. As the leader of the Slave Revolt, he seemed to me invincible. His role in this historic movement had been prophesied by Dionysus through Zagreus. He had astonished the world by defeating the Roman Army against all odds. Like many of his followers, I, too, felt there was something godlike about Spartacus.

In a last-ditch effort before the military season ended, Proconsul C. Cassius Longinus, governor of Cisalpine Gaul, thinking our army had been weakened by the loss of Crixus, launched an attack. He had expected a rout, only to find himself the latest to be humiliated in our series of victories. Spartacus sacrificed a goat to Nike, the winged goddess of victory.

At harvest time our warriors attacked nearby villas, freed the field slaves, and looted everything they could carry. Many of us followed to harvest the grapes, olives, fruit, and nuts, which we carried back to our wandering village in large baskets.

The Festival of Consualia marked the end of the harvest season with a holiday for beasts of burden. Horses, donkeys, oxen, goats, and sheep were fawned over like beloved pets, festooned with garlands, and treated to oats, carrots, and clover.

By the time we reached the foot of the Alps, it was late Autumn. The snow-capped, sixteen-thousand-foot peaks towered over us like a threat or a dare.

We were at an impasse. Everyone was unhappy. The people who had put their faith in Spartacus, had laid their lives on the line because they believed he would lead them to freedom, were having second thoughts. Many had been born in Italy. They didn't know the language of their ancestral homeland, much less the name or region or tribal village or clan from which their parents or grandparents had been captured. Others had been taken as prisoners-of-war from lands that touched the Mediterranean coast. Greece. Syria. Egypt. Numidia. Mauretania. Spain. Sicily. Crossing the Alps would only take them further from their homelands.

Pater was stricken with melancholia. Through her incantations and offerings, Mater beseeched Dionysus for guidance.

In mid-December Spartacus announced that we would wait until Spring to cross the Alps. The Roman Army had ended their fighting season and would not pursue us again till April.

Saturnalia was the biggest festival of the year. It was supposed to be in honor of Saturn, King of the Titans, whom the Romans regarded as their first king as well as their first god. Saturn learned from a prophesy that one of his children was destined to de-throne him. To avoid this, he swallowed each of his offspring as soon as they were born. But when his youngest son Jupiter was born, Saturn's wife wrapped a rock in diapers and tossed it down Saturn's throat, claiming it was their newborn. She sent Jupiter to be raised in secrecy by honeybees.

It was never clear to me why we celebrated Saturn, who was a terrible pater and had started a war against his own son. But I don't think anyone in the Army of Spartacus gave a thought to Rome's Golden Age of Kings and Titans. We were creating our own Golden Age of Freedom.

The holiday was officially supposed to last three days, but everyone managed to stretch it out to seven. The week was filled with feasts, music, and dancing. Competitive games and sporting events. We feasted on roast goat, boar, and venison. The Bakers made cinnamon honey cakes topped with nuts and dried fruit.

Potters and wood workers were kept busy molding and carving icons, small enough to fit in the palm of your hand, wear as pendants, or place on altars. Clay and wooden figurines of deities, mythical creatures, and animals. The Minotaur. Pegasus. Cerberus. Griffins. Dragons. Satyrs. Sphinxes. Athena's owl. Cybele's lion. Apollo's raven. The scorpion of Mercury. Peacock of Juno. Ant of Ceres. Eagle of Jupiter. Everyone gave and received so many of these icons that we used them as betting tokens when rolling the bones.

Mater's gift to me was a purple crystal vial hanging from a ribbon. The stopper was made of bone, carved in the shape of a woman's head. When I lifted it, an aroma of jasmine, honeysuckle, and gardenia wafted out.

Antigone smelled it and reared back. She took a second sniff, decided she liked it, and stuck her tongue into the slender opening.

"No, silly!" I scolded. "Don't drink it!" I examined the delicate head that formed the stopper. "This is Hope," I told her.

When Pandora released all the miseries it was possible for humans to suffer, only Hope remained in her jar. On statuettes, paintings, and jewelry, Hope was shown peeking out of, or emerging headfirst from, a vial or jar. I placed the ribbon around my neck. It seemed a good time to welcome Hope into my life. She was easy to forget. A shy, quiet being, nearly drowned in a sea of misery.

I sniffed again from the vial. It occurred to me that Hope is like perfume. Not something you can see. Not as easy to imagine as the flamboyant, egotistical gods, scheming of war and love and terrifying us with lightning and thunder and earthquakes and tidal waves. Hope cannot strike down one's enemies. Or curb hunger. Or heal wounds. The Romans believed Hope was a delusion, entertained by fools too cowardly to accept that reality is brutal and merciless.

To me, Hope felt like the glimmer of a brighter future. An imaginary ideal outcome that may never come to fruition. Something to keep me going when all else seemed lost.

With her marble-black eyes, Antigone peered into the emerald eyes of my Hope vial. I pressed one finger over the opening and tilted it upside down then upright, leaving a dab of perfume on my fingertip. I dabbed it on the indent of my throat and the top of Antigone's head.

"That we may always be reminded Hope is in the air. We may not see her. Or hear her. Or feel the force of her power. But we can sense the presence of her elusive aroma whenever despair threatens to suffocate us."

That night I soaked a daub of perfume into a scrap of linen and tossed it into the flames with a promise to Hope that I would never again forsake her. Each morning, I opened my vial and sniffed, to remind myself not to give up on the Future.

On the night of the Winter Solstice, Pater called upon me to gather Simon, who had turned fifteen in September, and Lucius, who had turned twelve, as well as Felix and myself, who were both thirteen, in his command tent.

"I wish you to cross the Alps and seek out the villages of Thrace, Gaul, and the Germanic tribes," Spartacus informed us. "To discover which regions have succeeded in fighting off Roman invasion. Which have been conquered. Which are still actively resisting."

He drew a map of the pass we were to cross over the Alps. How to find the River Isar and follow it northeast to the Danube River, then east along the southern bank, continuing as it cut south until the Rhodope Mountains came into view. We would have to ask locals to direct us to my parents' village. From there, if there was time, we should continue east to the Black Sea coast. On our return journey, we would follow the Danube back west along its north bank.

"Stop in the villages to commune with their wise men and women about the prospects of the followers of Spartacus settling in their lands," he told us.

We nodded solemnly, aware of the profound responsibility he had tasked us with.

"I expect you back by Summer Solstice," he said.

We had six months to complete our mission.

Part IV

ROMAN YEAR 439

WINTER–SPRING

18

Winter

After more than a year of trekking up and down the Apennines, I thought I knew mountains. But the Alps were a completely different beast.

As we climbed ever higher, the trees thinned out and grew shorter. Then disappeared. White-and-gray chamois with big dark eyes cavorted up and down steep, craggy slopes. Clusters of long-horned ibex moved elegantly across rugged terrain. Marmots stood on their hind legs and whistled when they saw us. Bearded eagles soared between the peaks, landing in nests balanced atop sharp spires. White-feathered ptarmigans with bright orange crests sauntered over the snow like royalty.

As we gained altitude the air became more difficult to breathe, leaving me lightheaded and dizzy. Not even Simon could explain this. But we all felt it. Were the gods testing us? Reminding us that our precious lives depended on ancient mountain spirits whose realm we had entered without invitation?

Some days we were enveloped in clouds of icy mist that hovered below the peaks. We stepped gingerly over crevices that descended into bottomless darkness. Waterfalls clung to deep fissures in suspended animation, as if commanded by Jupiter to "Freeze!"

I prayed to every god I could name to protect us from the path of an avalanche that could bury us in a matter of moments beneath hundreds of feet of snow.

Despite the treacherous terrain, I marveled at the beauty of this other-worldly realm. At times, the mountains were sublimely quiet, mesmerizing me into a state of profound serenity. It was like trekking through the land of the gods. Looking down into the valleys, I could see why it was easy for the gods to not care what tragedies befell the ant-like humans below.

"Follow the Dog Guard star, at the tip of the tail of the Little Bear constellation," Spartacus had told us. "He will lead you North."

Mater had given me an amulet of the Thracian Horseman Hero and a traditional Thracian outfit for my journey. An ankle-length wool cloak, woven in a pattern of zigzags, circles and dots, with a leather belt and wolf-faced silver buckle. Knee-high lace-up fawn-skin boots. And a pointy leather hat with rabbit fur lining, the front embroidered with the face of a fox. Perky foxlike ears stuck up from the top.

Antigone had grown longer and thicker. But she did not like the cold. Her skin turned the color of a frozen lake. She coiled around my neck in three loops, burrowing into the lining of the back and side flaps of my hat. Her eyes peeked out from beneath my left earlobe while her tail tickled my right ear.

At night, we lay wrapped in bear furs, staring up through the clear, frigid air into the night sky. All my life I had looked to the sky, searching for stars and constellations to guide me through the seasons. But I had never spent whole nights contemplating the indigo expanse of the universe. Gazing up at the stars inspired me to think Big Thoughts. What are the stars? I wondered. Who made them? How big are they? How far away? Does anyone live on the other planets? These questions led me to wonder about the earth. And how it came to be. And how old it was. Which led me to wonder how *everything* came to be.

I tried to piece together everything I had been told that could help me to answer these questions.

"In the beginning," I began, "was Chaos. An unmeasurable, unfathomable cloud of darkness, containing no life or land or water or substance. Darker than darkness. Silence so profound, the very concept of sound did not yet exist. A vast, mysterious *something*, composed of *nothing*."

Every child knew that first there was Chaos. But now it seemed impossible to imagine how *everything* could have once been an infinite mass of *nothing*. I paused, wondering if I had lulled my friends to sleep with my monotonous tone.

"Keep talking," Felix assured me. "We're listening."

"Out of Chaos were born two children," I continued. "Night, a black raven who embodied Darkness. And Erebus, a formless miasma. Night laid an egg in the arms of Erebus. Out of this egg emerged a golden-winged bird called Light. Light nurtured a spark that grew to become Earth. The Sky blossomed from Earth, like a flower from a seed.

"The first living creatures appeared in the space between Sky and Earth. Powerful beings called Titans took on a human-like form—though humans did not yet exist. But Sky was a terrible father. He hated his offspring and imprisoned them hundreds of miles beneath the surface of Earth, allowing only a dozen Titans to remain above ground. Saturn, angered by Sky's treatment of his brothers and sisters, attacked his father in a rage. From each drop of blood shed by Sky two new types of creature rose up. Giants and Furies."

"The three Furies went to live in the Underworld. The Titans drove the Giants from the Earth. Two Titans named Saturn and Rhea now ruled the Universe. Then Jupiter, their youngest son, rose up against them. Saturn and the other Titans went to war against Jupiter and his five brothers and sisters. Only one Titan, Prometheus, took the side of Jupiter. After Jupiter won this epic battle, he imprisoned the Titans in the center of the Earth. Seeing that Earth was now barren, Jupiter instructed Prometheus to create life forms to inhabit it."

"Kinda makes you think," Felix said.

"About what?"

"About everything."

"The philosophers refer to the boundless, infinite everything that exists as the *kosmos*," Simon commented.

"Pythagoras believed the entire *kosmos* is a single organism. And each of us might be a drop of blood in the veins of this infinite creature."

"Sometimes I feel like a drop of blood in a universal sea," Felix commented.

"How do you mean?" I asked.

"I don't know. I just do."

"Some philosophers say the entire universe is composed of only a few basic elements: earth, air, water, and fire," Simon continued. "Others claim even these fundamental elements are different combinations of indivisible, unseeable grains called *atoms*. They speculate that everything in existence is made up of an infinite variety of compositions of atoms."

"I can't picture it," I confessed.

"Imagine atoms are like grains of sand. And the universe is a vast beach. Each grain of sand is exactly the same. But they can be combined in an infinite variety of shapes and patterns to form every object and life form in existence."

"A world made of sandcastles?" Felix suggested.

"Yes. Plants, animals, and humans, all made from the same sand grains as everything else."

"Or snowflakes," Lucius suggested. "As if everything in existence is made from thousands upon thousands of snowflakes. And each of us is a snow-person."

"I'm so cold," Felix groaned, "I *feel* like a snow-boy."

It was the perfect image to lull us to sleep, ensconced in a world of snow and ice that was profoundly frightening yet marvelously intoxicating.

We trudged ever upward along a narrow ledge that descended hundreds of feet to a frozen river. The snow began to flurry. Within moments it was a blizzard. I could no longer see Lucius and Felix ahead of me. When I looked back, Simon had disappeared. I felt a surge of panic. Had the snow collapsed beneath their feet, sucking them into bottomless crevices? Had I been left alone in this stark, merciless world?

"Simon?"

"Right here behind you!"

"Felix?"

"Here!"

"Lucius?"

"Ditto!"

We clustered together, clasping each other by the shoulders. The sun was completely blotted out. We were enveloped in a world of whiteness. I was afraid we would be blown off the cliff.

"Get out your ropes," Felix said. "We'll tie ourselves together. Waist to waist."

The wind was so fierce, I could barely make out his words.

"We need to find shelter," Simon added. His deep voice resonated through the piercing wind.

"I'll take the lead," Lucius called.

We tromped through the blinding, deafening blizzard, tied together in a line. The icy snow stung my eyes and clustered on my lashes. Each time I planted my foot in Felix's tracks, I slipped downward.

"Here!" Lucius called out.

"Where?"

"What?"

"Right here."

I saw only more whiteness. No different from the wall of whiteness I had been gloomily staring at for hours.

"See?" Lucius insisted.

The wall of whiteness took on a milky-gray tone. Lucius stepped into it and disappeared. Felix followed, disappearing into the same void. It was as if they had stepped through an invisible door into a magical realm. I felt a tug at the rope around my waist. I stumbled forward, landing on my knees. Felix had pulled me in after him. Simon tumbled down next to me. We were surrounded by slick, hazy-blue walls.

An ice cave.

Lucius unpacked a clay lamp the size and shape of a hollowed-out hand, palm up, and set it on the floor. From a small amphora he poured olive oil into it then added a piece of tinder-fungus. He pressed his thumb to his fire-starter to flick the steel on one end against a shard of jasper on the other. Sparks fell onto the tinder and smoldered into a tiny flame that brightened as it soaked up the oil.

Deeper inside the cave, the whine of the wind was muffled. With our body heat, the air grew warmer. I removed my wool cloak. Sensing the change in temperature, Antigone stirred. Her pale-blue skin sprouted amber spots. We sat cross-legged around the dim flame. Felix fished a leather pouch from his satchel and poured a handful of midnight-purple berries into his palm.

"Prometheus," he began. "I offer this juniper berry in gratitude for teaching us the secret to fire, that your flame may lighten the darkness of this cave." He dropped a berry into the dish. "I would give you more, oh Prometheus. But our fire is humble and I'm afraid of snuffing it out."

"Amen," Lucius nodded.

"Amen," I echoed.

Simon intoned, "*Baruch atah Adonai, Eloheinu melech ha-olam asher kid'shanu b'mitzvotav v'tzivanu l'hadlik neir shel Shabbat.*"

"Is that your sacred language?" Lucius asked.

"Yes," Simon replied.

"What does it mean?"

"We praise you, Eternal God, Sovereign of the Universe, who makes us holy with mitzvot and commands us to kindle the Sabbath lights." Simon shrugged. "I have no idea if tonight is the Sabbath or not. But it seems like a good time to thank God for the blessing of light."

"Anyone want dried salt-fish?" Felix asked.

"Ugh!" we all groaned.

Before leaving, we had packed salt-fish, olives, nuts, dried fruit, and hard cheese. But we had finished our bread and cheese in the first couple days. The fruit, nuts, and olives not long after. Since then, we had lived on little else but dried salt-fish.

"Here." Felix poured Juniper berries into our cupped hands.

The texture was dense and chewy, the taste green and woodsy. As I chewed, a bitter citrusy undercurrent emerged. The aftertaste was sharp and spicy, a mixture of spearmint and black pepper. I offered one to Antigone. She swallowed it then hissed and coughed it up into my hand.

We rolled out our bear skins, covered ourselves with our wool cloaks, and used our bags as pillows.

"What you call Chaos we call the Chasm," Lucius intoned. "A vast realm of nothingness. North of the Chasm was the icy realm of Death. South of it, the realm of Fire. Twelve rivers flowed from the north into the Chasm, where they froze and became a land of ice. Clouds of fire drifted up from the south, turning the ice to mist. Drops of water from the mist transformed into the Frost Maidens and Ymir, the first giant. Ymir and one of the Frost Maidens had a son, who also married a Frost Maiden. Their son, Ymir's grandson, was Odin. Odin and his brother murdered their pater."

"Why?" I asked.

"I don't know." He continued, "From their pater's body they formed Earth. From his blood the Sea. From his skull the Heavens. With his eyebrows they built a wall to separate the realm of Life from the realm of Death. They gathered sparks from the land of fire and tossed them into the skies to form the sun, moon, planets, and stars. Odin created the first woman from an elm tree. The first man from an ash."

"Kinda makes you think," Felix said sleepily.

"About everything?" I asked.

"More or less."

Soon I heard the others breathing evenly. The light danced and flickered across the icy walls and ceiling.

"Kalysta," Simon whispered. "Are you awake?"

"Yeah. You?"

"Want to explore?"

"Sure!"

Bringing the lamp with us, we crept further into the cave. As we went deeper, the air grew colder and sharper.

I noticed a faint, brownish-yellow shape frozen into the wall at eye level. "Look!"

"What do you think it is?"

"Let's find out."

Simon held the lamp while I dug into the ice with my dagger, sending flecks in every direction until the tip of my blade tapped against it. I carved around it then pulled it out with my fingers.

A tiny starfish.

"Mater told me the whole world used to be at the bottom of a great sea, where giants bathed and frolicked," I said.

"There's your proof," Simon smiled.

"Here," I offered it to him. "You can have it."

"You keep it. You're the one who found it."

We continued ever deeper. As we descended into the heart of the mountain, I was overcome by a sense of desolation. I began to wonder if we had reached the outer edge of a realm of absolute nothingness. Something like the nothingness that existed before the universe was born. An ancient, soulless, absence of life.

I became afraid to go further. Afraid we were entering a realm of exile from all that lived and breathed.

"Do you think this is what the Underworld feels like?" I asked.

"The Jews don't have an Underworld."

"Where do you go when you die?"

"The Place Beyond . . ."

"Beyond *what*?"

"Life."

"But where is it?"

"In the Heavens, I suppose."

"Where the gods live?"

"Maybe," he shrugged.

He grew quiet. Then he said, "Is it okay if we sit?"

I spread my Thracian cloak over the floor and we sat side by side, our backs to the ice wall, the lamp on the floor in front of us.

I wondered if thinking about the Place Beyond made him sad. He had never told me much about his mater or how she died. Only that he remembered her saying prayers and lighting Sabbath candles.

"In the *Book of the Dead,* the Egyptians say that when you die, your heart is weighed, to determine if it is big enough to allow you into the Afterlife," he said. "The Jews believe when you die you stand before an angel, who asks: *Who are you?*"

"Who are you???"

"I think it means: Do you know yourself? What kind of person were you in life?"

"Like: *What is your character?*" I asked.

"Something like that. The Egyptians have a goddess, Maat, the embodiment of *Truth, Justice, and Integrity.* In essence, the same idea as the Stoics' *character* and the Jews' *Who are you?*"

He paused.

I knew him well enough to know that he had not yet finished developing his line of thought. And then I marveled that it's possible to know another person so well that you can sense the rhythm of their mind.

And I wondered if there are things about me - the way my mind works, or my moods, or the gods I turn to in various situations - that no one else knows me well enough to sense. No one but Simon.

"If your answer to the Angel's question is unsuitable, you may have to go to a place called *Gehenna*—a bad place—long enough to redeem yourself. After you have served out your sentence in *Gehenna*, you may go to The Place Beyond."

"Is it cold? Gehenna?"

"Some say it's a lake of fire. But my pater told me Egyptian Jews believe this because the Egyptians have a bad place for people whose hearts aren't big enough that's a lake of fire. That the Jews borrowed this notion from them. He told me *Gehenna* is not such a bad place as that - otherwise, no one would survive to advance to the good place."

He became profoundly quiet, and I knew he must be thinking of his mater.

Should I remain quiet, and allow him to be alone with his thoughts? Or was he hoping I would ask about her?

I had a realization that this was a moment in which I could *choose* to reach out to him. A month ago, my pride would have prevented me from so much as *entertaining* the idea of reaching out to touch Simon.

When our fingers were a hair's-breadth apart, resting on the ice between us, I placed my palm over the back of his hand. He didn't react but I felt certain that he welcomed my touch.

I squeezed gently.

He turned his hand palm upward and grasped my hand in his, gripping me with a feeling of need.

And then I had an *epiphany.*

Maybe Simon needed *me* as much as I needed *him.*

It sounds simple, but I had always only thought of him from my own inner perspective. Almost as if he were an object whose attentions I craved. But I had never thought that maybe *he* craved *my* attention as much as I craved his.

It was as if, for the first time in my life, I was able to step outside my own inner world to observe another person in a manner not directly related to my own needs.

My childhood selfishness - worrying about my own needs and wants and desires - had prevented me from appreciating that *he* also has an inner yearning for *me.*

As if my sense of self-importance to *myself* had prevented me from perceiving myself as important to another person.

I had been so worried that Simon would perceive me as wanting more from him than he wanted from me, that I had failed to appreciate that *his* desire for *my* affection might be as strong as *my* yearning for *his* affection.

I had been so preoccupied with wanting him to prove that he cared about me . . . that I had failed to appreciate his equal desire to be cared for *by* me.

These thoughts came to me as we sat in this antechamber to the Underworld, each grasping the other's hand, as if holding each other back from falling into an abyss.

"My mater made charm bowls," he said.

And I understood that he would not have told me he was thinking about her if I had not reached out to take his hand in mine. That he needed to feel the warmth of affection I had offered him, before he could talk about this person he had cherished and lost.

"Charm bowls are like curse tablets, except the words are painted on bowls rather than scratched into lead sheets. And they're more often wishes for good outcomes than condemnations of another person."

"She ran a little shop in Alexandria, next door to a potter. He made plain, shallow, unglazed bowls. She painted personal charms on them for customers who came to her, desperate for love or luck or health or prosperity."

I squeezed gently to let him know he could tell me more about his mater. That I *wanted* him to tell me more.

For I now understood that it's okay for me to want *more* from Simon.

That he *wanted* me to want *more* from him.

That he wanted *more* from me - whatever this ineffable *more* might turn out to be.

"I used to sit in her lap—I must have been two or three—while she reached her arms around me to hold the bowl in one hand and paint lettering on the inner and outer surface. I remember that she painted Egyptian hieroglyphs, because I would ask her what each of the pictures meant. The scarab. The feather. The bird. The woman keeling. The foot. The snake. The dog. The snail. The ibis. The ox horns. The eye."

As he named each image, he smiled an inner smile, as if picturing these hieroglyphs evoked long-buried feelings for his mater. As if each image resonated for him with a specific, precious, unnamable emotion.

"My Pater told me when I was older that she had painted charm bowls for patrons who were Egyptian, Jewish, and Greek. Everyone believed in the same spirits and charms."

He looked down and laughed lightly.

"Look," he said.

Antigone had wrapped herself around our clasped hands and was squeezing tightly, as if unwilling to let us separate.

"How . . ." I hesitated to ask, "did she die?"

"A disease of the Nile," he shrugged, as if the *cause* of her death were not important, so much as the *fact* of her death.

I squeezed his hand again, trying to absorb his sadness. Strangely, I had never before tried to feel what Simon might be feeling. Another symptom of my childish selfishness.

"But . . . I thought the Jews have only one god."

"One God. Countless angels, demons and unnamed spirits."

I shivered, as if a spirit had passed through my body. Antigone relaxed her grip, uncoiled herself from our hands, and spiraled up my arm to embrace my neck.

The lamp light flickered and went out. I sucked in my breath. Simon wrapped his arm around my shoulder.

"Are you afraid of the dark?" he asked.

"Not really."

We shuffled up from the depths of the cave. Simon was behind me, his hand on my shoulder, guiding me through the darkness.

"I'm sorry things got weird for a while," he whispered.

For a moment I hoped he would say more.

"It's no big deal," I said. "Anyway, it was a while ago."

For over a year I had been imagining a dramatic encounter in which feelings would be revealed and past slights remedied.

Instead, I got a vague apology.

I wondered if I had conjured a dark spirit in my own mind that never really existed. For all I knew, Simon may have spent the past year wondering why I had become so distant toward him.

Or, worse, maybe he *hadn't* noticed.

Before the breakout from the ludus, we had only ever seen each other for my tutoring sessions. Considering he no longer tutored me, there had been no reason to see each other at all.

And yet, he *must* have noticed the sudden distance between us. But, if so, why didn't he approach me to ask the reason for it? Why had he seemed to accept the sudden distance between us?

Until now.

Then he said, “You’re such a sweet girl. I didn’t want to . . . overwhelm you.”

I was grateful for the darkness that concealed my grin.

We hiked down the north side of the mountain and followed the Isar River to the Danube. If we were stopped by soldiers, we told them our fathers were fighting in their auxiliary army and that we had been sent to a nearby village to stay with relatives. If we were stopped by locals, we told them the Romans had sacked our village and we were on our way to stay with our clan in a nearby settlement.

Everywhere we found sections of Roman road, either already built or under construction. Clearly, they were intended for one thing only: Marching legions into tribal territories not yet brought under the yoke of Rome.

19

March

I stood on a slope of the Rhodope Mountains, overlooking my parents' village. My first impression was of eerie silence and the smell of charred wood. Burnt remains of fencing and stables sketched the outlines of two dozen cottages facing each other across a muddy thoroughfare. Chickens wandered in the wreckage, pecking hungrily at barren ash.

For two months we had walked hundreds of miles along the south bank of the Danube.

I had discovered that Thrace, Gaul, and Germania are not distinct regions or peoples, as the Romans imagined. When I asked locals what tribe they were from,

I had received answers such as, "My mater is Getai and my pater Thracian."

Or, "My mater is Scordisci and my pater Chernoles."

Or, "My mater is Dacien and my pater Boii."

There was no limit to the combinations of parental heritage I heard from the people I met, including those with three or four different tribes in their ancestry. All living together in the same villages.

I was certain Spartacus had no idea how far east the Romans had advanced. Numerous forts were under construction on granite hilltops that towered over the water. Slaves laying down long stretches of road announced the Republic's determination to rule the entire south bank of the Danube.

At a Celtic city called Esztergom, the river cut south. Eventually, we left the Danube, veering toward the Rhodope Mountains. At the Thracian city of Plovdiv, I had visited the Shrine of Dionysus, where Mater had been initiated as a Priestess. From there we had climbed the mountains, asking locals for directions to my parents' village.

While Lucius, Felix, and Simon explored the decimated cottages, I found the remains of my parents' home next to a fieldstone well. Nothing was left but the hearth, dominating the center of a single room. If I had been born there, Mater would have carried me three times around it in a ritual to introduce me to Vesta and symbolize my acceptance into the household under her protection. Just in case Vesta's spirit still lingered, I offered a prayer.

"Vesta, goddess of the hearth, please forgive us for allowing your fire to go cold. Mater and Pater will soon return and make offerings to your nurturing spirit." Then I remembered it's a bad idea to make promises to a god that you may not be able to keep. So, I added, "If they can."

"So, this is *home*," I said aloud. I felt no trace of the profound sense of attachment I had expected to overcome me.

This is the place Mater and Pater spent my whole life dreaming of? *This* is the one place they assured me I would always feel safe?

I tried to imagine my parents' cottage rebuilt as it had once been. I tried to imagine Pater roaming the hills with a herd of goats. It was hard to think of him living such a placid, uneventful life.

I tried to imagine Mater, tending the fire of Dionysus at the same hearth she used to cook meals. What would she do all day, with the wishes of only a handful of women to communicate to her god? I supposed she would spend it sweeping the dirt floor. Tending the kitchen garden. Feeding chickens.

And yet, this was the place I was expected to call *home*, for the rest of my life? What would I do here? There was no marketplace, teaming with vendors and traders, suffused with the aromas of roasting bread, exotic perfumes, fresh-cut roses, and mulled wine. No streets to run through, carrying messages and prayers and tinctures and baskets of offerings. No private tutor to wile away the afternoons.

How would I spend my time? I could run from one end of the village to the other and back in less time than it would take to name all twelve of Hercules' labors. I supposed I would marry an illiterate shepherd and spend my days sweeping the dirt floor. Tending the kitchen garden. Feeding chickens.

What will Mater and Pater do when I tell them their village has been razed to the ground? I wondered. *They will still want to return. To gather their scattered kin and rebuild. Arm themselves to defend it from the next onslaught of Romans.*

Would I go with them, to spend the remaining days of my life here? And if I didn't, where would I go? I could never go back to Capua. But . . . *this* place?

The realization that, from before my birth, Mater's most profound wish had been that I would one day return to my ancestral village depressed me. How had she not known that, growing up a thousand miles away, this village would never hold the same meaning for me that it did for her and Pater?

Lucius joined me. "You're finally home," he sighed. "I wish I could say the same."

I envied him, having a home that existed in his own memory. A place where he had been born and spent his childhood. For me, *home* in Thrace had never been more than a nostalgic tale, woven from my parents' rose-tinted memories.

"How far is your village from here?" I asked.

"My village no longer exists," he said. "It was destroyed by a hostile tribe, mercenaries for the Romans. But a village to me is not a home."

"What do you mean by home, then?" I asked.

"Home is wherever my clan is."

"How will you find them?"

"I will find them. And fight beside my fellow clansmen to keep the Romans from occupying a single jugerum north of the Danube."

Simon joined us.

"Is there a place you would call home?" I asked. "In Egypt?"

"I was five when Pater and I were brought to Capua," he replied. "I have vague memories of my mater singing prayers and lighting the Sabbath candles, before she died. I remember playing at Pater's feet in the Library. I remember being on a ship. I remember the pirates. But I have no memories of Alexandria as a *place*."

"If you could go anywhere," I persisted, "to settle, where would it be?"

"I don't think it's so much a *place*. Home for me would have to be somewhere there are people around who I can talk to about ideas that interest me."

I had never thought of home as anything but a specific location. Could home for me be anywhere I was among fellow Thracians? I didn't think so. Besides Mater and Pater, I felt no closer to Thracians than to anyone else. Lucius was Zarubintzy. Simon was Egyptian-Jewish. Felix Mauritanian-Celtiberian. I had felt more at home in an ice cave on top of a mountain, hunkered down with my friends, than I ever would in a Thracian village. Could home for me be any place where I'm among cherished friends?

Felix joined us.

"What's your idea of home?" I asked.

"A place where I can paint all day and sleep all night."

Beyond the far end of the village, I followed directions Mater had given me to a cave entrance hidden from view by a tangle of blackberry bushes. The others waited while I crawled through the low, narrow mouth and continued crawling down a passageway until my hands and knees touched damp earth. Here the tunnel opened into a circular room with a ceiling of crystal amethyst. Holes had been drilled down from the ground above, creating skylights that illuminated the sacred room with columns of sunshine.

I stood and stretched my back. An image of the Three Water Nymphs, holding hands and dancing, had been carved into the rock and painted in bright colors. In the center, three springs filled a whirlpool. The floor of the pool was covered with layers of offerings. Brooches. Amulets. Rings. Charms. Scarabs. Perfume vials. Icons, carved from bone, glass, shells, amethyst, and amber. Bronze and silver bells and coins. Frog, mouse, and bird skeletons.

I pulled the starfish from my bag.

"I make this offering to the you, Water Nymphs . . ." I hesitated, unsure what to say next.

Mater's refrain, "In the end, all the gods can offer us is Hope for the Future," resonated in my mind.

". . . In hope that, a thousand years from now, a girl will see this starfish and honor you with her own offering. And pray for your eternal protection of these springs."

On my knees, I leaned forward to scoop a sip of the sacred water. Antigone dipped her head in, slipped from my arm, and disappeared beneath the surface.

"Antigone!"

Had she accidentally loosened her grip and fallen in? Did she dive in on purpose? Did she know how to swim? Had the whirlpool sucked her into an underground cistern?

"Antigone!"

I buried my face in my hands. Would I never see her again?

She reappeared, gliding across the surface and frolicking in playful spirals.

How had I forgotten that Mater had first met Zagreus as a baby snake, swimming in this very pool? That she had visited the shrine of the Water Nymphs as a girl many times before the snake of Dionysus chose to twist its body around her arm and bind itself to her soul?

No wonder Antigone was so happy. This was her ancestral home.

"I'll miss you, Antigone," I whispered.

With my eyes closed, I dipped my fingertips into the water.

A fluttering at my wrist. A light pressure squeezed my arm. It spiraled up to my shoulder and around my neck, where Antigone nestled into the fur lining of my fox-hat flaps.

Maybe she decided home to her is wherever I am.

Somewhere along the Danube, Felix and I had turned fourteen. With such a formidable mission before us, it hardly seemed worth mentioning.

20

Spring

We reached the shore of the Black Sea on the night of the Spring Solstice. Then followed the coastline north for about a week and cut northwest until we caught up with the Danube. In villages along the north bank, we met people of the Suebi, Marconni, Quadi, Cimbri, and Teutoni tribes.

In a village that specialized in apricot trees, we feasted on apricot stew. Apricot bread. Apricot custard. And apricot honey-cakes.

Their Priestess showed me an ancient icon of a red fertility goddess.

"Who is it?" I asked.

"No one knows," she said. "I found her in the river mud as a girl. Because she chose me, I was recognized as the High Priestess. I was no older than you at the time."

When she saw Athena's owl tattooed on my back, the Priestess insisted on giving me a tiny owl icon carved from purple fluorite. Antigone licked the surface with approval. The Priestess dropped a sticky ball of herbs and spices mixed with apricot tree sap into her mouth. Her skin shimmered in a rainbow of colors.

"It will fill her veins with Hope for the Future," the old woman said. "Now, tell me, girl. Who is this Spartacus, whose name rings up and down the River? Is he man or god? Or merely a wishful rumor?"

"He's very real," I said.

She handed me a hot spiced apricot drink and sat beside me at her hearth. "Tell me everything."

"Everything?" I asked.

"How did this Slave Revolt begin? They say it was prophesied by a Priestess of Dionysus. Is that true?"

I told her about the prophecy. The breakout. Mount Vesuvius. Our victories. The split with and defeat of Crixus. The impasse at the foot of the Alps.

By the time I finished, dawn was breaking. The Priestess took me to watch the sunrise over the river. Light reflected off the water like a silver pathway to the Future. Antigone's skin sparkled like diamonds.

"You must live to tell the story of the Rebellion," the Priestess said. "To bear witness to the Legend of Spartacus."

She gave me a gold coin with a gladiator on the face and the words: Spartacus Victorius. The obverse featured Dionysus with a snake and the word: Prophecy.

"Where did this come from?" I asked. "Surely, it wasn't minted in Rome."

"We people north of the Danube mint our own coins," she replied. "We're not quite the barbarians the Romans make us out to be."

Lucius learned that his clan had resettled after being pushed north. At a juncture where a tributary branched off from the Danube, he told us, "My clan was last seen following this waterway."

A gray-coated beast the size of a colt bounded toward us from upstream, its teeth bared. I froze like a rabbit facing down a fox. Felix dove sideways into the river. Simon stepped slowly backward.

The creature lunged at Lucius, knocking him backward. He was pinned to the ground, only his arms and legs visible beneath his attacker.

"Lucius!" I tried to pull the rabid animal off before it killed him.

"No!" Lucius cried. "It's okay."

The gray beast was ferociously licking his face. Lucius wrapped his arms around the dog's back, hugging it close and nuzzling its neck.

"Off," he said sternly.

The dog stepped back and danced about, wagging its tail and barking with joy. Lucius stood up and brushed the dirt from his back and legs.

"Sit," he said.

The dog did as it was told.

"This is Loki," Lucius told us.

I approached gingerly. Felix emerged, drenched, from the river. Simon joined us. Antigone stretched to touch noses with the dog.

"He's been waiting for me," Lucius explained. He patted the dog's head. "Haven't you, Loki?"

Loki barked happily at being recognized for his loyalty. I was reminded of Argos, Odysseus' dog who waited twenty years for him to return from the Trojan War.

"This is where the Romans ferried me and the other captives across the river," Lucius said. To the dog: "You knew I would return, didn't you?"

Loki barked and wagged his tail.

"It's been more than a year," Lucius explained. To the dog: "You've been feasting on wild hare all this time. I see how plump and satisfied you've become."

We knew by then that Lucius was leaving us. We also knew that, as a warrior, he would tolerate no heartfelt tears. No dramatic speeches. No profound expressions of friendship.

I gave him a curse icon I had bought from a villager. It featured an Evil Eye being attacked by a lion, an ibis, a snake, a scorpion, and a wolf.

Felix gave him a statuette he had carved of the three-headed man-monster-god.

Simon told him, "I know you will live a good life because your decisions are wise, courageous, and just. You always *do the right thing*, no matter the consequences."

Already heading down the trail with Loki frolicking at his heels, Lucius turned to raise his fist.

"Peliculosam Libertatem!" he called out.

We raised our fists.

"Peliculosam Libertatem!" we echoed.

21

Late Spring

The journey south across the Alps in June was much easier than crossing north in the dead of winter. Less of an adventure into the unknown. More of a mission to return and report our findings. With longer hours of sunlight, we put in longer days of hiking and spent less time contemplating the universe. We talked less, conserving our breath.

The Alps in summer offered its own stunning beauty. Meltwater gurgled beneath the ice, cracking and booming like thunder. Larch, stone-pine, spruce, birch, and beech trees, bursting with fresh green growth, huddled below the timberline. The air was heavy with the perfume of wildflowers. The bees, drunk on nectar, hummed contentedly.

Antigone was determined to eat one bloom from every type of flower we encountered. White edelweiss, lace-flowers, and snowbells. Yellow buttercups. Rusty-red Alpen-rose. Orange primroses. Stormy-blue gentians and forget-me-nots. The lavender spines of Lupine and delicate purple faces of bellflowers. Vanilla orchids with blood-red veins.

Each time she swallowed a bloom, her skin changed to match its color. I soon understood that she found this game amusing and was trying to entertain me with her playful transformations.

We sat in my parents' tent, describing what we had seen over the past six months. It was a hot night and the sides had been rolled up to for a breeze to pass through. Apicius prepared a special meal to welcome us back. Meat balls baked in gravy spiced with pepper, lovage, and cumin. For dessert, spelt pudding boiled in raisin wine with dried pears, topped with crushed, roasted hazel nuts and honey cake crumbs. I gave Pater the gold Spartacus Victorius coin that had been minted in Thrace and gave Mater a carved stone icon of the Thracian Horseman Hero.

Spartacus nodded and listened, nodded and listened. He cried when he realized the devastating truth. Much of Thrace had been decimated. And Roman incursion into Thracian and Celtic territories was more extensive than he had imagined.

"If it were only the three of us," he gestured to Mater and me, "I would say, Let's go back to Thrace–whatever's left of it–and join the fight to drive the Romans from our lands. When I broke out of the ludus last year," he continued, "I believed I was one man with the simple goal of returning with my wife and daughter to my home. I could not have dreamed I would be joined by tens of thousands who would come to depend on me for their futures. I have sixty thousand people counting on my leadership. I've brought them this far. I cannot abandon them now. I must see this thing through to the end."

"Ah, but husband," Mater smiled indulgently, "you *did* dream it."

Zagreus unwrapped herself from Mater's arm, stretched to Pater's shoulder, and wriggled toward his throat until she had wrapped herself three times around it, as if to remind him of the prophesy and strengthen his resolve.

I had never seen Pater so sad. Though only thirty-one, he seemed to me an old man. In his troubled face, I saw the tragedy of a person who will never again see his home.

I asked myself if Capua, the only home I had ever known, pulled at my soul in the same way Thrace tugged at the hearts of Mater and Pater. I had enjoyed my mornings in the marketplace. I had relished running to the ludus to visit Pater and receive his bear-hugs. I had cherished my afternoons outside the city walls, leaning against the willow tree with Simon, a scroll between us, the lazy brook at our toes. I had loved my evenings in the Temple with Mater and Zagreus by the blazing fire of Dionysus, inhaling the pungent aromas of magical herbs.

But even my happiest memories of Capua were tainted by the scourge of slavery. The slave auctions in the marketplace. Kids as young as Lucius, sobbing in their shackles. Women with babies in their arms, roughly pawed by strange men. Men, separated from their families and sold to the ludus, where they faced no future beyond death in the arena. Even if I could turn back time to the day before Pater's escape, Capua would never again be home to me.

"What other options are there?" I asked.

Spartacus thought for a long while. "We are merely a hangnail on the toe of Rome. In the final battle, we will surely lose. And yet some of our warriors are for returning south to attack the city of Rome."

"Didn't Crixus already try that?" I asked incredulously.

Pater shook his head. "For some, the defeat of Crixus has only emboldened their thirst for revenge."

"Or," Mater suggested, "we can head south to the tip of the boot, where we can try to find ships to take us across the Strait of Messina to Sicily."

"Why Sicily?" I asked.

"Sicily has had three slave revolts in the past fifty years," Mater explained. "There are slaves there who remember the most recent uprising. And whose parents and grandparents remember earlier rebellions. They may be awaiting a new leader to inspire a new generation to rise up against Roman rule."

"It would be easier to take and hold a small island than an enormous peninsula," Pater added. "And Sicily is the breadbasket of Rome. Their army depends on Sicilian grain. If we can control the grain trade, we'll have a valuable bargaining chip to convince the Romans to settle with us."

"Why didn't you think of that in the first place?" I asked in frustration. "The tip of the boot is only a hundred miles south of Capua. We have journeyed six hundred miles north. And now you turn us back to travel seven hundred miles south?"

"Do you have a better idea?" he asked.

Later, by the fire, I whispered to Simon, "I can't believe he's going to make us walk all the way to Regium."

"Remember Aesop's Fable about the Fox and the Cat?" he replied.

"I think. That's the one where the cat and the fox are talking about which of them is smarter. The fox thinks he's clever because, when he's running, he can dart back and forth, pivot without warning, and scurry through brambles. The cat admits his only defense is climbing trees. Then a pack of hunting dogs comes upon them.

The cat climbs a tree and is safe. But the fox, no matter which direction he runs, is caught in the end." Then I added, "I feel sorry for the fox. But I'm not sure what that has to do with us."

"The cat has only one move, but it saves his life," Simon explained. "The fox has a dozen moves, but none of them save him. Spartacus has a plan—to take us to Sicily. Would you rather we dart back and forth across Italy until the Romans catch us?"

Pater held a vote on the question of whether to cross the Alps and join the tribes fighting off Roman invasion. Or travel south to Regium, seeking passage across the Strait of Messina to Sicily. With a lot of grumbling and expressions of frustration, discouragement, and weariness, the vote was in favor of Sicily.

On our way South, Felix and Vitalio left us to go to Pompeii. The Pictor Imaginarius of a home decorating firm there had seen Felix painting the Spartacus mural and invited him to work at his studio. Felix had not confessed to being a runaway but the man had explained that he could have freedman's papers written up with no questions asked. He offered Felix work in his shop painting murals in the homes of rich people. After seven years, the man promised, Felix would be free to do as he pleases.

"In seven years, I'll be twenty-one," Felix noted.

"What will you do then?" I asked.

"Probably keep working for him. Or start my own decorating business."

"Felix thinks the Pictus Imaginarius will help me to find work at a Blacksmith's shop," Vitalio added. "With no questions asked."

I was sad to say goodbye to my friends. But they promised we would one day see each other again. After the Rebellion succeeded and we were free to travel without worry. I envied them, having made a decision that led to a future where they would soon feel at home.

Part V

ROMAN YEAR 439

SUMMER–AUTUMN

22

Summer

I loved living on the beach!

Mornings, I joined the other teens, swimming and romping in the crystal blue waves. Antigone uncoiled from my arm to swim alongside me, catching sardines in her mouth. At low tide, we built sand sculptures of our favorite gods. Then watched them dissolve from the feet up as the tide came in.

Afternoons, we rowed out with the local fishermen's children and learned to catch giant tuna. On shore, Apicius taught us to gut, debone, and slice them into steaks and grill them over driftwood bonfires. He made a sauce of pepper, cumin, coriander, lovage, wild onion, and wine, drizzled over the fish and topped with roasted hazelnuts. I tossed my first bite into the flames, offering gratitude to the Three Graces: Splendor, Mirth, and Good Cheer.

Nights, we sang folk songs in Celtic, German, Thracian, Ostian, and Latin. We lay in the sand and gazed up at the Milky Way, the path walked by gods between earth and Mount Olympus. The bright nose of Orion's hunting dog heated the earth, bringing us the sweltering Dog Days of Summer. When a brilliant green meteor streaked across the sky, I felt certain it was a sign from Fortuna that we would be able to stay here, free from Roman aggression, for the rest of our days.

After two-and-a-half years of trekking and fighting and fear, we breathed a collective sigh of relief. Our wandering village was sequestered along three miles of beach. Behind us, the Rough Mountain rose sharply to its rocky peaks. Our shepherds grazed their flocks on a grassy slope that rose up from the coastline. To the southeast lay the Ionian Sea. To the northwest, the Tyrrhenian Sea.

Dirt roads at both ends of the beach, too narrow, rough, and uneven for a Legion on the march, led to the Via Annia. The Romans, now under General Crassus, had taken a break from pursuing us. Things in the Senate, we heard, were contentious. Our ongoing Rebellion had put the Patricians in a bad mood.

Two miles across the Strait of Messina, Sicily beckoned. Light from the rising sun reflected off the colossal gold shield of the Athena statue that stood on a hill above the city of Messina. Soon, she would welcome me in her golden embrace.

"It seems so close," I told Mater. "I feel as if I could swim there."

Mater warned me of the murderous waters that lay between the two points of land.

"A sea monster named Charybdis lurks beneath a fig tree on the Sicilian shore. When Charybdis inhales, she draws in massive quantities of water, sucking into her gullet any boat that crosses her path. When she breathes out, the waves rise to huge heights, submerging any ship that dares sneak past her. The motion of the water, sucked in and spit out with each breath of the sea monster, creates whirlpools into which countless men and ships have disappeared."

"On the Italian side of the Strait," Mater continued, "sits Scylla, who leans down to crush men and ships between her jaws as they try to pass. Her six heads hang from six necks that undulate like giant snakes. Each of her six mouths has three layers of shark teeth."

"If a ship veers too far west," she concluded, "it will be drowned in the whirlpools of Charybdis. If it veers too far east, it will be crushed between the jaws of Scylla."

I remembered Scylla and Charybdis from a passage in Homer's *Odyssey.* When Odysseus's ship entered the Strait, Scylla crushed it in her jaws. Charybdis swallowed six of his men. Hercules was left floating on a raft. Then Charybdis swallowed the raft and Odysseus was left clinging to a tree for dear life. When the monster belched up his raft, he continued safely to the other end of the Strait.

Around this time Simon turned sixteen. And, while I was still fourteen, for once our age difference didn't seem quite so significant.

Tavia, now sixteen, and Plutus, who was seventeen, were married on the beach. She worked for weeks to weave her wedding tunic and veil from yellow wool. Mater helped to tie her ewe's-wool belt in a Herculean knot. I braided daisies into her hair and scented it with essence of gardenia.

Before a fire, Plutus took Tavia's right hand in his, kissed it, and placed a ring with an intaglio of the Bee Maiden on her finger. She removed her veil and they faced each other, holding hands. He spoke his vows so quietly I couldn't hear the words. Tavia concluded her own vows with, "We are two souls of a single spirit."

We tossed pistachios at them, shouting, "Feliciter!"

Together, they lit a torch of white pine, in honor of Ceres. Tavia had baked a special grain cake, which she and Plutus broke in half and tossed into the fire. A pig was sacrificed and roasted. To avoid a bad omen if she stumbled, Plutus carried Tavia to their new tent.

One afternoon, I found Pater playing pan pipes in the pasture that rose up from the beach. His plaintive music had attracted the goats, who grazed around him as if they would follow him anywhere. He spoke in low, soothing tones and fed them from his hands.

Pater was always somber these days. To his followers, he was a brilliant general, an undefeated warrior, and a great leader. Almost a god. I tried to reconcile this image with the realization that my Pater was, at heart, a humble shepherd, the most peaceful and gentle of men.

I knew things were bad. That we were backed into a corner. But I had never been happier.

"I wish we could live here forever!" I exalted.

"Orpheus," Pater began, as I sat beside him, "was the son of the Muse Caliope and the King of Thrace. When he played his golden lyre, animals, trees, and even mushrooms danced to his ethereal tunes. His beloved wife Eurydice was killed by a snake bite, kidnapped by Pluto, and imprisoned in the Underworld."

"Orpheus risked his life to descend to the land of the dead and beg that Eurydice be allowed to return to earth and live with him. 'Eurydice will follow you,' Pluto assured him, warning, 'Do not look back until you have both reached the surface.'"

"Orpheus safely set foot in the land of the living. But, afraid Eurydice had fallen behind, he glanced back. He missed her so dearly he could not bear to wait another moment. At that moment, she dissolved into thin air and was sucked back down to Hades. Orpheus never saw her again. When he died, his lyre was placed in the sky as a constellation."

I nodded. Legends of the gods were supposed to contain depths of wisdom. But I often failed to see the lesson in them.

"The past is an illusion," Pater explained. "It dissolves into thin air if you are foolish enough to believe you can bring it back from Oblivion."

So, Pater was like Orpheus. And Thrace was his beloved Eurydice. If he became distracted from the

Rebellion by his longing for his homeland, he would lose sight of the future of those who followed him.

It struck me that, many times, Pater must have been tempted to awaken Mater and me in the night and steal off with us to cross the Alps and make a home once again in Thrace. Only the knowledge that he held the fates of sixty thousand people in his hands prevented him from giving in to his longing for home.

"If we stay," he concluded, "The Romans will crush us from both ends of the beach, slaughtering us in the sand or forcing us to flee into the sea and drown."

If the Romans forced their way through the narrow gaps between mountain and sea on either end of the beach, we would indeed be trapped. There would be no chance to melt into the wilderness, as we had done so many times in the past. The mountains that sheltered us from attack also prevented us from retreat. The rocks were too craggy and the cliffs too steep to climb. Propelling down a five-hundred-foot cliff by rope was one thing. Scaling to the top of a thousand-foot cliff was an impossibility even Spartacus couldn't think his way into.

I perceived more than ever that Spartacus wished he were not the leader of a Rebellion. I wondered if he regretted taking to heart the prophesy that had sparked his defiance of Rome. Did he blame me, for bringing him all the kitchen knives? Should I blame myself?

But I couldn't regret my choice. I understood by then that I am the kind of person who does not stand idly by while others are suffering. And that Pater, too, did not regret the Hope he had inspired in so many.

"I need you to take a message to Crassus," he said.

General Crassus had been sent to accomplish what six legions failed to do. Wipe out the Army of Spartacus and put down our Rebellion once and for all. The Senate had given Crassus unlimited power to do "whatever it takes" to snuff out the Slave Revolt. His fresh legions had constructed their garrisons along the Via Annia where it met up with the beach road.

Already, a Century from the army of Crassus had engaged in a skirmish with a band of our warriors. And lost because their men dropped their weapons and ran in fear. This minor victory only emboldened our warriors and made them even less inclined to listen to the voice of reason, which assured them the day would come—sooner than later—when the Romans would triumph over us.

Three days later, a contingent of our army met that of Crassus on a field. This time it was our warriors who fled. The first defeat of the Army of Spartacus since the uprising.

We learned afterward that Crassus had inflicted a terrible punishment on his soldiers who had fled in the previous skirmish. He had ordered a Decimation, an ancient military punishment that had not been practiced for hundreds of years because of its barbarity. It required that one man from each tent-unit be chosen by lottery as the victim. And that his fellow squad-mates beat him to death with wooden clubs. Any man who refused to participate would himself be beaten by the others.

Now the Roman soldiers were more afraid of their own general than of the "barbarians" in our slave army.

"Run to the north end of the beach," Pater instructed me. "Take the road about five miles to the entrance of the Roman garrison. Tell the sentries you are the daughter of Spartacus. That you have a message from me. That you will meet the son of Crassus under the rocks that overhang the point where the beach ends and the road begins. That you will be alone and unarmed. That he, too, must be alone and unarmed."

23

September

I don't know what I expected. But the son of Crassus was not it.

He arrived on a mighty war horse with red ribbons woven into its mane and a jeweled harness, as if decked out for a parade. The horse was too big for him and he had trouble dismounting. He was clad in the regalia of a Roman officer, which appeared to be a size too large for him. He wore a golden helmet that covered his face, with holes for the eyes, nose, and mouth. Its stylized silver hair resembled Medusa, twisting out from his head like snakes. To match, his breastplate was molded with the face of the snake-haired Medusa stamped into it. It was so highly polished that the sun glaring from his chest nearly blinded me.

Standing at a distance, he portentously removed the helmet.

The son of Crassus was short, with dark hair. He must have been thirteen because he still wore a bula, a bronze neck-ring with a pouch full of charms that, by tradition, would have been given to him by his mother. This would be removed when he turned fourteen in a family ceremony to mark his entrance into adulthood.

"I am Tribune Publius Licinius Crassus, son of General Marcus Licinius Crassus," he announced.

I almost laughed. He spoke louder than necessary, as if he'd been practicing this introduction. His tone was overly formal and full of pomp, considering he was addressing an unarmed, barefoot girl, arms and legs encrusted with sand, the hem of her tunic damp with salt water. And probably smelling of seaweed.

"I am Kalysta, daughter of Spartacus the Thracian and the High Priestess of Dionysus," I called back.

He approached in stiff marching steps.

We stood face to face.

His silver scabbard was molded in the shape of the Wolf who nursed the twin boys Romulus and Remus at the founding of Rome. On his fingers were three rings with oversized gemstones carved in the likenesses of Hercules, Mars, and Achilles. A gold eagle brooch clasped his red wool cloak at one shoulder.

I couldn't help thinking he must be sweating something awful, trapped in all those layers of bronze, silver, gold, and wool.

"What is the message?" the son of Crassus demanded. He sounded irritated, as if the task of conducting a war parley with a slave girl was beneath a soldier of his status.

"Spartacus offers Rome a peace treaty. His army will cease to harass Rome if Rome will grant an unsettled territory where our sixty-thousand former slaves may live as freedmen."

"Is that all?" the son of Crassus asked disdainfully.

An hour later, he returned with his pater's reply.

"No."

The next day, Spartacus sent me with a second message.

This time, as the son of Crassus removed his golden helmet, he caught my eye and smiled. As if he had forgotten for a moment that I was his enemy.

I was thrown off guard by his smile, which didn't at all match his stiff, formal speech of our previous encounter. It took great fortitude to remind myself to hate this person I didn't even know. This spoiled rich boy who had been groomed from the cradle to treat slaves without an ounce of humanity.

To cover the awkwardness of trying not to smile back, I stood stiffly and recited my message in what I hoped was an official-sounding tone.

"Spartacus challenges General Crassus to one-on-one combat to the death."

I waited for a reaction worthy of Spartacus's challenge. But his face was rigid and unreadable.

"He asks Crassus to recall that a Sicilian slave revolt was once resolved when a Roman general agreed to face the rebel leader in a duel," I continued. "If Crassus slays Spartacus, the slaves will return to their former masters—with a written promise that they not be punished. If Spartacus slays Crassus, our community of escaped slaves will be allowed to remain in this coastal basin. We will pay what taxes are due to the Republic, given we are allowed to live here as freedmen. Why sacrifice tens of thousands of lives on both sides, when we could resolve this issue with the death of one leader?"

Again, the answer came back. A resilient, "No."

Before I turned back to relay this answer to Spartacus, the son of Crassus blurted out, "Why do you have that snake on your arm?"

Antigone, her skin seaweed green, was stretched languidly around my arm, her head cradled in my palm, the tip of her tail tickling my earlobe. On hearing her name in an unfamiliar voice, she stretched her neck to gaze at the strange boy.

"She chose me as her soulmate." The son of Crassus didn't react as I had hoped, so I added, "She is the daughter of Zagreus, the sacred snake of Dionysus who has bound herself to my Mater."

"The Priestess of Dionysus?"

I nodded and stepped closer. It seemed we were no longer arch enemies, foot soldiers of opposing generals, but new acquaintances, curious about each other.

"It was her prophesy that sparked the Spartacus Revolt," he said.

Antigone stretched her head toward his hand in a friendly way.

"Does she bite?" he asked.

"I don't know," I said. "I've never met anyone foolish enough to give her a reason to bite them."

He stepped back. I couldn't help enjoying the sense of power it gave me to strike fear in the heart of a Roman soldier. Even if he was only thirteen and the pampered son of the richest man in Rome.

"During the Civil War," the son of Crassus began, "my family backed Sulla. When his side lost, my uncle and grandpater were assassinated. My mater and pater fled to Spain. They hid in a cave for three years. I was born there."

"You were born in a cave?"

He nodded. "But I don't remember it. During Sulla's Second Civil War, my pater was instrumental to his winning the Battle of the Colline Gate."

"Your pater is a remarkable man," I said. I didn't mean to be sarcastic. But I was afraid it came out sounding that way.

"Have you heard of Gaius Julius Caesar?" the son of Crassus asked.

"No."

It seemed each time I thought our conversation was over, he was desperate to keep it going. I wondered if it was lonely in the garrison with no one his age to talk to.

"Caesar is a friend of my pater and a rising star in the Senate," he added.

"I don't exactly read the gossip notices about what's going on in the Senate," I admitted. This time I meant to be sarcastic.

"Caesar says I'm an up-and-coming young man. He promised to recruit me as his military adviser when I come of age."

I was not a big fan of bragging. Especially about feats you hope to accomplish in the future. At least wait till you've actually achieved something before you go around tooting your own horn.

"You're lucky!" the son of Crassus blurted out.

Talking to him wasn't so much having a conversation as responding to a series of blurts.

"You get to swim and fish and camp on the beach. I'm stuck in a garrison five miles from the coast," he said, sounding like a little kid who resents not being invited to a birthday party. "Your pater doesn't command his soldiers to beat one another to death with clubs," he added.

"That must have been horrible to watch," I remarked, genuinely sympathetic.

"It was." He looked down at his sandaled feet, as if ashamed of the memory.

"Then join us," I said.

And immediately regretted it. If he were to walk with me into our encampment, he would immediately be seized as a prisoner of war and interrogated until he revealed Crassus' strategy. Or held hostage and used as a bargaining chip.

The son of Crassus paused, seeming to consider my offer. Then he shouted into my face, "I would rather *die* than take up with a hoard of filthy barbarians!"

His spittle flew into my eyes. Antigone bared her teeth and hissed. Her skin flared fiery red and sprouted menacing black spots. For a moment I feared she might bite him. Not that he didn't deserve it.

That night around the bonfire, Simon said, "The Jews believe there was once a place where food was plentiful. Everything was easy. There were no fears or worries or disease or wars. It was called the Garden of Eden."

"Sounds like a nice place," I said.

"I fear our lives will never again be as full of splendor, mirth, and good cheer as this summer has been," he murmured.

I, too, wanted these blissful, carefree days to go on forever. But always, at the outer edges of our beachfront village, the army of Crassus lurked.

Over the following weeks, Spartacus took a rowboat out to the merchant ships that appeared along the coast, to meet with their captains. He asked if they would consider ferrying loads of escaped slaves to Sicily. I was surprised to learn that we had accumulated a treasure of coins and jewelry. He offered this treasure to any admiral of a fleet willing to carry us across.

Week after week, he was turned away. The merchants were afraid of reprisals from Rome, if they were caught aiding the Slave Revolt.

Mater stood over her brasier, entreating Dionysus to send us ships. In reply, Dionysus gave her only Hope. My own Hope vial was down to a few precious drops.

24

October

One evening I entered Spartacus' Command Tent to find him sitting with a strange pointy-bearded man. He wore a sleeveless leather tunic with long strands of fringe hanging from the hem and neckline. His thick hair was styled in braids that clung tightly to his head. A string of gold coins shone forth from his skin.

The stranger smiled as if he recognized me.

"I have just learned that a certain lion, who was supposed to be half-starved, greeted me in the arena with a belly full of goat meat," he said.

"The Lion Tamer?" I asked in astonishment.

"The very same."

"I didn't recognize you with a beard," I admitted. "As far as the lion, I know nothing about that," I grinned.

"Of course you don't," he winked.

I sat and listened as they got down to business.

"I've invited you here," Spartacus said, "to ask if you can see a way to transport us across the Strait to Sicily."

"How many are you?"

"Sixty thousand."

Heraclio smiled. "Between the jaws of Scylla and the lungs of Charybdis."

"We do not need to sail in comfort," Mater noted.

"If it were up to me, as a brother gladiator and former slave, I would gladly take your band of runaways to Sicily. But a pirate captain is beholden to his crew. Like you, I am their leader. Not their master. That said, my men are no friends to Rome. The Senate recently committed funds to carry out a crackdown on piracy."

"I have heard," Spartacus nodded.

"On the other hand," Heraclio continued, "My men owe loyalty to no man, country, or philosophy. They are motivated only by the promise of wealth. And mischief."

"I'm not asking that they do this out of the kindness of their hearts," Spartacus assured him. "Or to make the world a better place. Or for the good of humanity."

With each phrase Pater uttered, Heraclio nodded, confirming that his crew of pirates indeed had no stake in *doing the right thing*.

"We offer a treasure, plundered from wealthy villas throughout Italy," Spartacus added.

"I would like to see this fabled treasure."

Pater stood and removed a tapestry he had been sitting on to reveal a bronze chest, reinforced with snake-shaped iron bands. Silver tiles on each side were set with multi-colored gems indicating the stars in the twelve constellations of the Zodiac. Pater used a ring on his finger, which turned out to be a key, to unlock the chest. An explosion of color lit the tent with a million sparkles.

Heraclio leaned in to get a closer look. So did I. Necklaces, rings, bracelets and earrings, encrusted with garnets, emeralds, amethysts, agates, diamonds, peridot, black pearls, jasper, sapphire, and amber, filled the chest. Not to mention countless gold and silver coins.

"You are a rich man, Spartacus."

"We own it collectively," Pater assured him.

"You are a good man, Spartacus."

Pater allowed the brilliance of the treasure to sink in.

"I have calculated it would take a fleet of twenty-five to fifty ships to transport everyone across the strait in ten round trips," Spartacus told the pirate.

Hercalio nodded but said nothing.

Spartacus closed and locked the chest then replaced the tapestry. "Please stay and share a meal with us."

I was sent to tell Apicius that Pater had a special guest. I returned with four plates of grilled sea scorpion and turnips in a cream-sauce of cumin, saffron, and sesame seeds. For dessert Apicius himself brought a hazelnut, honey, and pepper custard, molded in the shape of a ship.

"My dear Apicius," Heraclio laughed, greeting the head chef with a hearty hug. (You've haven't been truly hugged till you've been hugged by a gladiator!) "My only regret in freeing myself from the bondage of Batiatus was that I would forever miss your fine cooking."

"Please, join us," Heraclio, Spartacus, Mater, and I all said at once.

"Don't mind if I do." Apicius scooped a generous serving of custard onto a plate he had brought for himself.

I felt it was finally an appropriate time to ask the question that had been burning on my lips since first recognizing Heraclio.

"What happened to the lion?" I asked.

"When I left Capua, I asked that the lion be transported with me to the port of Ostia, where we gained passage on a merchant ship headed for Africa. From the port of Tripolitania, we walked into the wilderness to the cave where I first found him. There I set him free. He soon returned with a freshly killed gazelle. I built a fire and enjoyed my roast while he gnawed on his share raw. I explained that it was time for him to create his own family. After many fond pets and much slobbering on my face, he strode back into the wilderness. I found passage on a coastal ship bound for Numidia."

"How came you to captain a pirate ship?" Spartacus asked.

"As Fortuna so deemed, the ship that was to carry me home was captured by pirates. They put me in chains and threw me into the hold with their other captives, to be sold at a slave market in Spain. I was so downhearted, having twice already been captured and sold into slavery, I came close to hurling myself into the sea. Then I thought better of it. I had heard of the Spartacus Revolt and thought, if one man can stand up against the Roman Republic, surely, I can outsmart a band of pirates. I let word get round that I was the famed Lion Tamer and demanded to speak with the Captain."

"When I was brought on deck, I challenged the Captain to one-on-one combat. He was understandably hesitant to take on a former gladiator. What would the captain of a pirate ship have to gain from a dual with a captive slave? You might ask. Pirates become captains based on the fear and respect of their fellow sailors. For the captain to deny my challenge would be to admit that there may be a man more worthy than he of leading these men. His crew would never again respect him. Still, he hesitated."

"To sweeten the deal, I told him I would fight with my legs and arms still in chains, if he would fight bare-handed. I added that, if I were to win, I would be made the new captain. The crew cheered at this suggestion. Now he had no choice but to take me on."

"I will spare you the blood and gore—you've seen enough to last fifty lifetimes. Suffice to say I used my shackles as my weapon. On seeing their former leader defeated and bleeding on deck, the men wanted to throw him into the sea. I told them to set him in a lifeboat with enough food and water for a week. If the gods wished to spare his life, no doubt a passing ship would take him on board. Most likely for the purpose of selling him into slavery."

Heraclio agreed to take Spartacus' proposal back to his crew. Before leaving, he turned to me. "I owe you a life, my dear girl. Perhaps one day I will be able to repay you. Until then," he removed a gold coin stamped with a giraffe from the chain around his neck. "I wish to honor your good deed with this token."

After he left, I added the coin to the ribbon with my Hope vial.

A woman poked her head into the tent, beseeching Mater for help with a birthing. I was about to leave when Pater bade me to stay.

"Did I ever tell you you're descended from royalty?" he asked.

I giggled.

"I'm perfectly serious."

"I thought your family were shepherds."

"My pater—your grandpater—*became* a shepherd. But he was born a prince. His pater was the last in a line of kings dating back four hundred years. He was descended from Teres, the first King of the Odryssians, a coalition of tribes that ruled much of Thrace. You are also a descendant of Alexander the Great, who married an Odryssian princess, daughter of King Kotys, who is my ancestor."

"What happened?" I asked.

"Our kingdom was conquered by Mithradates VI, Poison King of the Black Sea."

"I've heard of him."

"In truth, my grandpater surrendered to Mithradates."

"Why didn't he fight harder for his kingdom?"

"Mithradates was an unstoppable force. He had united several kingdoms in the Anatolian Peninsula to fight off Roman invasion. King Spartacus knew it would be better for his people if he surrendered peacefully than to get them killed fighting for a lost cause. Besides, he would rather be a subject of a remarkable Asian king than a victim of the ruthless monster that is Rome."

"Out of respect for his royalty, Mithradates recruited my pater, who was fourteen at the time, into his army. During this campaign, my pater met and married a woman from the Dii clan of the Bessi tribe. After he left the military, he moved to her native village in the Rhodopes and learned to herd goats. Not long after, I was born. Your Mater and I were playmates from childhood and married as soon as our parents would allow us."

"Why are you telling me this?" I asked. "I mean, why are you telling me *now?*"

"I don't know how this will all end. But in case something happens to me and your Mater—"

"Nothing will ever happen to you!" I interrupted. "You're a demi-god."

He laughed. "Would that it were true. May the gods protect us! But I want you to know where you came from."

It wasn't clear to me what to make of this astonishing information. Somehow it was easier to accept the notion that my pater was part god than to imagine he was the son of a prince.

"Kings and kingdoms rise and fall," he explained. "Treasures are won and lost. Then won again. One day you're a prince; the next day you're a shepherd. One day you're a gladiator and a slave; the next day you're the leader of a rebellion; or captain of a pirate ship. Fortuna never reveals her plans. You cannot predict where on her Wheel you will land next."

His words made me somber.

"Cheer up!" Pater smiled. "It's not over yet. Freedom may yet prevail—against all odds."

"Dangerous freedom?" I asked.

"All freedom is dangerous."

25

October - December

I ran to find Simon, who was finishing an evening meal with his students. He had turned sixteen in September, and, while I was still fourteen, it seemed that, finally, our age difference no longer mattered—regardless of whether we were one or two numerals apart.

When we were alone, I told him of our hope that Heraclio and his pirates would transport us across the Strait, in exchange for the treasure.

"But Heraclio's men haven't agreed yet," I added. "What will we do it they don't?"

Simon thought about it. "Why not build our own ships?"

"Spartacus already thought of that," I explained. "No one in our community is a ship builder. The locals will not help us build ships for any amount of money. They're afraid of the consequences from Rome if they are caught aiding the Rebellion."

"Okay maybe not ships. What about rowboats?"

"Fishing boats?" I asked.

"They can't be hard to build."

"I don't think more than eight people could fit in one of those. Maybe ten. Tops. We would need to build at least six thousand."

"Or six hundred," Simon mused, "if each boat made ten round trips across the Strait and back."

"Six hundred boats is still a lot."

"We could make six thousand trips in one boat. Or six hundred trips in ten boats. Or one hundred trips in six boats. Or sixty trips in a hundred boats," Simon calculated.

"Ten boats seems doable," I agreed. "Maybe sixty."

"What's the harm in trying?"

"If Felix were here, he would have one designed and built by morning."

"We can copy the fishing boats the locals use. If it's seaworthy, we can show it to Spartacus and see what he thinks," Simon suggested.

"There's plenty of wood from shipwrecks and broken boats washed up ashore," I said. "One of the local girls told me a general once ferried a hundred elephants across the Strait on rafts build from driftwood."

"Let's start tomorrow. We can work on it in that cove at the east end of the beach. No one needs to know until we're finished."

"And until we've proven it seaworthy," I added.

Luckily, time was on our side. The Roman fighting season had ended and would not begin again till Spring. It took weeks to gather enough driftwood and boat scraps. We borrowed saws, hammers, and nails from the Carpenter, refusing to reveal our secret project.

Every morning before working on our boat, Simon and I stood at the top of the highest hill, scanning the horizon for the purple sails of pirate ships.

No purple sails.

The Bear Guard joined his fellow constellations. Each morning, the waves were choppier and the water colder.

No purple sails.

The Seven Sisters disappeared below the horizon. Nights grew longer. The sea more often stormy than calm.

Still no ships.

Orion disappeared from the night sky. Only the most intrepid among us insisted on fighting the irritable waves to swim out as far as we could. Each dawn, I stood on the beach, gazing across the Strait at the colossal bronze Athena, her golden shield reflecting the sunrise. I carved votive dolls from driftwood and swam out as far as I could to release them, hoping they would find their way across the water and somehow land at Athena's feet.

"Athena, protector of sailors, I offer you this doll as proof of my devotion. The owl on my back demonstrates my commitment to your example of *metis*. Please bring Heraclio's fleet of pirate ships to this shore and see that they safely transport us to freedom in Sicily."

When I had sent out fifty dolls, I began to lose hope.

"What if Heraclio never comes?" I asked Mater, as she stood over her brazier.

"He will."

"But what if he *doesn't*?"

"Heraclio will not betray us."

The Eagle star appeared, signaling the deadliest time of year for sea travel. The icy waves turned ominous gray-green and rose to ferocious heights. Neptune's moods swung from brooding to hostile to murderous, his trident poised to impale any fool who dared take him on.

By mid-December, we had completed construction of a six-person rowboat. We borrowed brushes and paint to give our seacraft a cheerful sky-blue coat. Antigone changed colors to match.

On a full moon night, we met in our secret cove to test it. We built a fire on the beach to guide us back. Simon took first turn sitting with his back to the bow to row while I sat at the stern, facing forward.

The waves were relatively calm but murderously deceptive, concealing the deadly rip tides. I had seen four people sucked down from waist-deep water and carried out to sea along these hidden currents, never to be seen again. Not even their bodies washed ashore.

We took turns rowing until the lights of the port of Messina appeared equally distant from our own fire. Then we lifted the paddles and sat side-by-side on the center slat, munching on a midnight feast of bread, cheese, and grapes. Antigone unhinged her jaw, demanding that I feed her one grape at a time until she looked like a string of giant blue pearls.

"Do you think we could make it all the way across?" I asked.

"Maybe," Simon said. "But what if something happened and we couldn't return? Everyone would think we had drowned."

"Or what if we capsized and drowned before we reached the other side?" I added.

We were quiet for a long time. The boat was rocked by the water, lulling me into a state of serene contentment.

"This breeze is soft as honey," Simon whispered, his loose black curls glossy in the moonlight.

I felt a delicate touch on the tender side of my lower arm. Simon had grasped it so gently I could sense more than feel his fingertips. He clasped my hand in his. Our fingers interlocked.

Then he said, "Your smile outshines Aphrodite's."

26

20 December

The following morning, I awoke to find the peaks of Rough Mountain white with snow. Antigone wrapped herself around my throat in a frigid collar and turned sickly green. Simon wrapped his arm around my shoulders and squeezed me to his side.

Three purple sails appeared on the horizon. A ship.

Six purple sails. Two ships.

Nine Purple sails. Three ships.

Twelve ships.

Fifty pirate ships!

We ran down to the beach, shouting.

"The Pirates are here! The pirates are here!"

"Pack your bags for Sicily!"

"Say goodbye to Italy!"

People gathered on shore to see the glorious ships that would carry us to freedom. Gilded masts swayed above the decks like votive dancers in purple robes. Silver-plated oars glinted in the sunlight like mermaids skipping across the waves.

Our treasure chest was loaded onto a fishing boat. Pater and two of his warriors rowed into the waves, heading for the bow of the flagship. A cluster of men stood on deck. I caught a glimpse of bright red above one man's head. It resembled the red feathered crests that topped the helmets of Roman officers.

I shaded my eyes with my hand to make sure it wasn't the glare playing tricks on me. *It must be Heraclio,* I thought, *wearing a Roman helmet as a joke. Or to show off that he has conquered a navy fleet. As soon as Pater climbs aboard, he and Heraclio will laugh about it.*

Spartacus's boat drew closer to the bow of the flagship. A string of transport boats appeared from behind the other ships in the fleet, heading for shore. The pirates would load our people onto these boats and deliver them to the ships.

But something was wrong. They were already full of people.

Soldiers!

Hundreds of longboats, filled with thousands of soldiers. The red crested man at the bow of the flagship was a Roman Navy Admiral.

The Lion Tamer had betrayed us. These were not pirates. They were Romans!

Spartacus and his guards were so focused on reaching the flagship they didn't notice. The wind picked up. The waves grew choppier. The transport boats were closing in on the beach. I had to warn Pater to turn around. Not to hand over the treasure. But he was too far out. My voice was drowned in the crash and whistle of the wind and surf. I splashed in and swam furiously, scrambling across the waves. In the frigid water, my muscles clenched. My arms felt weak and rubbery. Antigone clutched my arm, stiff as a corpse. It was not long before I caught up to them. Pater reached out to help me in.

"Decided to join us?"

"Romans!" I blurted out, panting breathlessly.

Thousands of soldiers were stampeding through the surf. Their trumpets blared insistently, driving them further inland. Pater and his rowers struggled to turn around, paddling with all their might. But these former gladiators were not skilled oarsmen.

I moved to the stern, trying to stay out of the way. A wave washed over my head from behind. When it pulled back, it took me with it.

My cries were drowned in the clanging of javelins against shields. Trumpets blaring the call to charge. The battle cries of thousands of soldiers. The screams of thousands of men, women, and children rose above the melee.

Spartacus dove into the water and swam toward the shore. The boat tipped. The treasure chest tumbled into the sea. His guards scrambled to follow him.

I struggled to stay afloat. A wave lifted me up. When it pulled back, I was sucked down by a powerful force. My lungs filled with water. I was disoriented, uncertain which direction would lead me up to fresh air and which would send me deeper into Neptune's murky graveyard. A mermaid wavered into view, as fluid as sea water.

I felt myself being hauled up by two large hands, gripped under my armpits. I gave a silent prayer of gratitude to Athena for saving me from the clutches of Neptune. I coughed up salt water and wiped my eyes with the back of my hand.

"We caught one!" the man who had pulled me out now held my neck from behind in the crook of his arm.

Antigone squirmed down to my wrist, squeezing so tight in her fear, my hand went numb.

On shore, Spartacus charged through the surf and disappeared into the melee.

"What should we do with her?"

"Throw her overboard."

"Feed her to the sharks. I hear they love slave girls.'

That got a laugh.

"I'm not a slave!" I shouted.

"Pardon me! You're a Patrician Domina."

"The daughter of Crassus."

"Pompey's cousin."

"The Pharoah's sister?"

They roared with laughter.

"I'm a free woman!"

The man holding me in a headlock grabbed my left arm and twisted it behind my back. "You don't look so free."

"She fell off the boat that was heading for the flagship," one of them pointed out. "She may be valuable."

It was decided that I be taken to the flagship, a trireme with three levels of oars, the bow curved up to a masthead of Minerva. On the prow a giant eye had been painted to ward off the evil eyes of enemies, pirates, and sea monsters. I counted thirty oars on each level, ninety men on each side, all of them slaves.

I was handed up a chain ladder from man to man, like a sack of grain, and deposited on deck, where I landed on my hands and knees. I tried to stand but my legs were weak and shaky. A circle of men gawked at me as if they had dredged up a mermaid.

"What good is she to us?" a soldier asked snidely.

The man with the red-feathered crest, the Captain, rubbed his chin. "I'm not sure."

One of the soldiers jumped back with alarm. "She's got a snake!"

Poor Antigone turned the color of a bruise and tucked her head into the creases of her body. Playing dead.

"Antigone is a sacred snake of Dionysus."

"Is your mater per chance the Thracian Lady?" the Captain asked. "The one who prophesied the Spartacus Revolt?"

If I said *Yes, I'm the daughter of Spartacus and the Thracian Prophetess,* would they plunge a sword through my chest, right there and then? Would they torture me to reveal Spartacus's strategy? Or hold me as a prize captive and take me to Rome, to be paraded through the Forum? Or thrown into the arena for Death by Devourment?

If I said, *No?* Then what? I was just another slave girl. They might toss me overboard without a second thought. Or sell me to the next pirate ship that came along.

"She's weighing her options," the Captain smirked. "Trying to decide if she will fare better by saying Yes or No."

Then I had what Simon called an *epiphany*. Whether I lied and said *No*, or told the truth and said *Yes*, would be a reflection of my character. This could be the last choice I would be given the freedom to make. If my life were to end at this moment, would I die with the confidence that my final decision had been wise, courageous, and just?

I decided to tell the truth.

"I am Kalysta, daughter of Spartacus, Freer of Slaves," I pronounced, wondering if these would be the last words I ever spoke.

I glared at the Captain, hoping I looked fierce. Defiant. Indomitable. I was certain I looked like a drowned rat. Antigone valiantly flashed sunset-orange.

"Hmmm!" the Captain grunted. I had expected him to be more impressed. But of course, he assumed I was lying.

"My Mater is a Priestess of Dionysus. Her prophecy launched the Slave Revolt," I added, wondering if *those* would be the last words I ever spoke.

On shore, thousands of soldiers stampeded up the beach toward the hills. A wall of bronze backs moved inland. Foot soldiers poured in from both roads. The screams of my people, struck down as they fled, flowed over the waves. Hundreds of bodies littered the blood-drenched sand.

I wondered if Simon was still alive. After spotting the sails, we had run in different directions, announcing their arrival. Had he been among the first to be struck down by Roman spears?

Those who had been further inland might have had time to run into the hills before the murderous tide of soldiers reached them. Mater's brazier was near the base of the cliffs. The bakery, too, was far back from the water. Tavia may have dashed into the hills before the soldiers reached her. Plutus had probably been training fresh warriors. He would have turned to face and fight the Romans, to protect those who were fleeing.

I was grateful that Lucius, Vitalio, and Felix were hundreds of miles away.

"They will disappear into the mountains," I assured the Captain. "You will never find them." It seemed I could not yet guess what would be the last words I spoke in this life.

He regarded me shrewdly. "Do you know who I am, daughter of Spartacus and the Dionysian Prophetess?"

"You're a Roman and you have no idea how it feels to be a slave."

"True," he conceded. "Nor do I care to imagine the mindset of an inferior humanoid. Have you heard of General Gaius Julius Caesar?"

"No," I assured him. But the name sounded familiar.

"Maybe not. But one day I guarantee you will see my face on a gold aurei."

He removed his helmet and set it at his feet. He looked young and fresh-faced, no older than thirty. His expression was amiable, with no trace of the cruel, stern lines I would have expected in a military leader. He wore a bemused smirk, as if he found everything amusing because he was confident that, whatever the game, he would win in the end. That, like a cat, whatever misfortune befell him, he would land on his feet. And, like a cat with a mouse under its paw, he was in no hurry to kill his prey.

He leaned back against the railing, his elbows propped on the edge, like a man at a pub, launching into a long discourse for the edification of his fellow drunkards.

"Not long ago, I was bound for the island of Rhodes, to study rhetoric and oratory, when my ship was captured by pirates. I informed them of who my family is and convinced them that taking me to Rome and ransoming me back to my pater would fetch an infinitely higher price than they could get from selling me in the slave market. I only had to show them the fine rings on my fingers to convince them."

Caesar displayed the same set of rings I had seen on the son of Crassus: Hercules, Mars, and Jupiter, etched in emerald, ruby, and topaz. One on each of the three central fingers of both hands. I remembered that the son of Crassus had told me of a certain General Caesar.

"The pirate captain happened to be a runaway slave," Caesar continued, "a former gladiator, granted his freedom with the honorary title of Lion Tamer. If I were Batiatus, I would not have been so merciful. Look what his show of leniency got him? That very night, his entire ludus rose up against him. The pardon of Heraclio gave those two hundred gladiators a vision of freedom. Nothing less could have inspired them to risk such a reckless act of defiance."

I felt compelled to correct this arrogant Roman. "They broke out of the ludus because a Prophesy of Dionysus proclaimed that Spartacus was to lead a great rebellion," I protested. "He is the son of Athena," I added.

"Ha!" Caesar scoffed. "I doubt you believe that. Such superstitions prove the weak intellect of the slave mind. This so-called prophesy is pure political propaganda, perpetuated by Spartacus to brainwash his followers into believing his false promise of freedom."

He gestured to the beach, where thousands of bodies lay slaughtered, their blood caught by the tide, staining the foamy crests of the waves red. He continued his story, confident the snuffing out of the Spartacus Slave Revolt would go on as planned, without his help.

"For the next three nights I was treated by Heraclio and his pirate crew as an honored guest. They wanted to return me to my family in good shape. To demonstrate that they had earned my ransom. Before I stepped off their ship and into the boat that would take me to my family waiting in the port of Ostia, they slapped my back and bid me farewell as if we were brothers. 'You will see me again soon,' I promised. 'When I return to capture every last one of you scoundrels and slit your throats with my own dagger.'" He paused to give me time to be impressed. *"That* is what I think of showing mercy to one's enemies."

"Spartacus will lead his people to freedom. No matter how merciless you are," I blurted out.

"Look!" He gestured to shore. "Your pitiful slave army is being squeezed from both ends. Those cliffs are too steep to climb. Even for Spartacus."

I wanted to shout, *Spartacus will never be defeated!* But Pater had been right all along. The Roman military could not be beaten. We had won many battles. But we had lost the war.

"Imagine my good fortune," Caesar continued, "when, three days ago, while sailing home from a battle to put down the rebellious Poison King, I came across the very same crew of pirates that had captured me months earlier. My interrogations revealed that they were on their way to transport sixty-thousand runaway slaves across the Strait of Messina. That, in exchange, they were to receive a magnificent treasure, the accumulation of three years of looting from hundreds of villas throughout Italy."

"The treasure lies at the bottom of the ocean," I assured him. "I saw it fall in when Spartacus dove from his boat."

"I saw it, too," Caesar shrugged. "No matter. I hear you've met the son of Crassus."

I was shocked to learn that he had heard of me at all.

"Talk about a foppish fool!" he snorted.

If I hadn't been so thoroughly devastated, I would have laughed at the accuracy of his description.

"I guarantee, history will not remember the son of Crassus." Caesar paused, scrutinizing me. "But you, now. There's something in you. An inner fierceness. Resilience. *Metis*. I suspect you may well live to make your mark on history."

I had no fight left in me. My heart felt as if it were sinking to the depths of the Underworld. I rushed to the railing, grabbed hold of the edge and hoisted myself up, prepared to dive into the waves. Not because I held any hope. But because my hope had run out. I would either swim to shore and be cut down by a Roman sword. Or drown before I got there. Either way, this nightmare would soon be over.

I had always wondered why the River Lethe, which I would have to cross to enter the Underworld, caused the newly dead to lose their memories of who they were and what they had experienced in life. Now I imagined the state of Oblivion as a mercy. I couldn't bear the idea of being haunted for eternity by the horror of that bloody beach.

Caesar's powerful hands grabbed me by the waist.

"Hold on, girl!" he said in a deep, calm voice, pulling me back from the brink. "That is not your destiny." He held me firmly while two of his men shackled my hands and ankles. "You're like a lion cub," he laughed. "More courage than sense."

I felt hollow. Drained of all thought, speech, or will to live.

"Throw her in the brig," Caesar ordered. "With the Lion Tamer."

27

20 - 21 December

A soldier grabbed my elbow and roughly escorted me below deck, not caring that, with my ankles shackled, I couldn't walk down steps. I stumbled like a limp puppet as he dragged me behind him.

He opened a door, revealing a bearded man, hands and feet shackled, sitting with his back against the wall. I was shoved into darkness, falling face down. Dank sea water sloshed across the floor. The door was bolted shut. The soldier's footsteps mounted the stairs and clomped across the deck.

"Heraclio?"

"Kalysta! My dear girl! What are you doing here?"

"Pater was on his way to your ship with the treasure. I saw the Roman transport boats. I thought you had betrayed us. I swam out to warn him. They stormed the beachhead. I was picked up and taken here. My people have been slaughtered."

"I suppose Caesar told you he intercepted our fleet and executed my men?"

"He bragged about it."

"Come here, my dear girl."

I scootched across the floor to sit next to him.

"I'm sorry it has come to this. I had high hopes for the Spartacus Revolt."

I could feel my face contorting as if I were about to cry. But no tears came.

It was all over. We had lost. Tens of thousands who had put their faith in Spartacus lay slaughtered on the beach. Thousands captured. Hundreds might have escaped into the mountains. But it would have been a rugged climb. Only the strongest and most nimble could have made it.

"What will he do with us?" I asked.

"Caesar? Nothing good, I'm afraid."

The pitch-blackness oppressed me. Panic filled my veins like venom. My tongue was coated with salt water.

My chest tightened. I breathed in shallow gasps, fighting for air. A silent wail arose from the depths of my soul.

Antigone was stiff and motionless. She was a brave little snake. But, like me, she could only handle so much terror and anguish and helplessness before her senses shut down.

Everything was lost. The freedom of sixty thousand people. Pater, cut down or fighting for the lives of his followers. Perhaps captured and even now being taken to Rome, to be paraded through the streets to the Forum, where he would be executed before thousands of cheering citizens. Mater, possibly escaped but more likely cut down or captured.

There was nothing to say. We sat in darkness for hours. I drifted into merciful sleep.

I was awoken by commotion. Transport boats knocked against the hull of the ship. Trumpets blared triumphantly. Countless pairs of sandals tromped across the deck. Soldiers shouted, drunk on Victory. Men's voices called out orders to hoist the sails. The anchor chain groaned and knocked against the hull as it was lifted through the water and hoisted on deck by the cranking of a giant spindle.

A man shouted to the oarsmen to take position. A drumbeat called them to action. The Bosun's voice chanted:

Hey, men!

One-hundred-and-eighty men echoed his words while dipping their oars into the waves and pulling them back to force the paddles forward. They groaned as they lifted their oars then pushed forward to swing the paddles back.

Shout back your echo . . .

Again, the oars were dipped, pulled back, lifted and pushed forward:

with a resounding Hey!

One-hundred-and-eighty men groaned and grunted as they dragged the boat through the stubborn waves, their raw muscles the only force moving us forward. The floor rocked and swayed as we headed out to sea.

Under our sliding weight . . .
the conquered waves . . .
are helpless . . .

"Where are they taking us?" I asked.

"Probably to the port of Ostia. And by transport up the Tiber River," Heraclio replied.

I needn't ask what would become of us.

With the force of our Hey! . . .
our sturdy prow . . .
cuts the waves like a dolphin's nose

Heraclio shook his head sadly. "I'm afraid there will be no honey cakes on silver platters or crystal goblets of violet wine to greet us at the gates of Rome."

Stirred by our strokes . . .
the sea foams . . .
like a rabid dog . . .

I don't know how long we sat in that dark room, rocked by waves and lulled by the drumming and chanting and grunting of the oarsmen, the dipping and pulling and lifting and pushing of oars.

The bolt slid across the door. Light poured into my eyes like vinegar. Two soldiers grabbed Heraclio and jerked him to his feet. A third dug his fingers into my shoulder and yanked me up. We were shoved up the steps and onto deck.

It was dusk. We were in the middle of the Strait. No other ships were in sight. The brisk wind was refreshing. Antigone stirred on my arm.

Was this the end? Were we to be tossed overboard like undersized fish? I wondered if Antigone would uncoil herself from my arm and swim away in search of her own destiny.

We were brought before Caesar. I hated his self-satisfied smirk that said, *Once again, everything has turned out exactly the way I wanted it to.*

"Over fifty thousand bodies lay rotting on your beloved beach," he informed us. "Over six thousand prisoners taken live. Perhaps several hundred escaped into the mountains. Rome suffered no more than a few dozen casualties."

There was no arguing that we had been utterly defeated.

I wondered if the son of Crassus had killed anyone. I doubted it. Most likely his pater had kept him safely behind the lines of action. I hoped he might live to become a better man than his pater.

"What of Spartacus?" Heraclio asked.

"Official reports claim he was slain on the beach. A spear pierced the artery in his thigh. He was surrounded and cut down."

"How do you know it was Spartacus?" I asked. There seemed to be nothing more to lose, no matter what I said.

"Six eyewitness accounts."

"If they had known it was Spartacus," Heraclio assured him, "they would have brought his head to Crassus as proof."

"True," Caesar conceded. "But no matter. The Rebellion is over. Rome has prevailed. Many generations of slaves will be born and die before another revolt plagues our Republic. Tonight, the senators will sleep well for the first time in two years."

I wanted to spit out a defiant retort. To contradict his proclamation. But I, too, knew it was over. Head of Spartacus or no head of Spartacus. After the slaughter on the beach, no slave in their right mind would dare to hope Spartacus still lurked somewhere in the mountains.

Heraclio and I stood helplessly, awaiting the pronouncement of our fate. I glanced westward to the setting sun. The statue of Athena stood in shadow, seeming to shrug, as if admitting even she couldn't rescue me from the clutches of this arrogant young general.

I thought of Antigone, the young woman from the Sophocles play. Brave as she was, when led in chains to be sealed in a cave, she couldn't help pitying herself for the future she would not live to see.

Caesar stood at the prow, looking out. "Bring them here."

Our bodyguards did as they were commanded.

"You see that?" He pointed to a black chunk of rock that jutted up from the ocean, flat and triangular on top, about six feet above the surface. The waves crashed violently against it from all sides.

"Dead Man's Rock," Heraclio murmured.

We were ordered to climb down the chain ladder into a rowboat. One man held the oars. Another pressed a dagger to my throat, his rank breath hot in my ear. The third aimed the tip of his sword at Heraclio's chest.

The boat bobbed in the waves and knocked against the hull. It was clear we were to be left on the rock to meet our fate.

"Why leave us here?" Heraclio called up to Caesar. "You would achieve far more glory by taking us to Rome. The Great Caesar, Capturer of Heraclio the Pirate and the Gladiator's Daughter, child of Spartacus. No doubt you would be honored with a Triumph."

"Gaius Julius Caesar, direct descendant of Venus, will not go down in history as the man who ended a Spartacus Revolt. I will leave that honor to lesser men like Crassus. I am destined for a grander legacy. I will be known as the man who conquered Spain, Gaul, Germania, and Britannia. Perhaps Asia, Egypt, and the Levant at well. The man who made Rome the grandest empire the world has ever seen. The Roman Alexander the Great."

"I'll be watching your career with interest," Heraclio smirked.

The tide picked up. The boat rocked precariously in the churning waves.

"And you, girl," Caesar called down to me. "You should die proud to be the daughter of a champion gladiator and a brilliant, unparalleled general. Your mater, on the other hand, is a harpy. The one they call Celaeno"

Harpies are winds from the Underworld, birds with women's faces, who carry people to their deaths and leave a foul smell in their wake. Celaeno, the Dark One, is the most powerful.

"She's not a harpy!" I shouted. Apparently, I had a drop of fight left in me.

"Dionysus is a foreign god from the East. Any woman who worships in his cult is a harpy. You are the daughter of a powerful harpy. Possibly the one they call Stormswift."

"Then why not throw me overboard?" I asked. "Why set me on a rock?"

"It will not be said that Caesar is a man foolish enough to kill such a powerful harpy. Nor will it be said that I am fool enough to spare her life. I leave it to Neptune to carry out your fate."

"I must ask you one last question," Heraclio called up. "The day you were returned to your family and my crew claimed your ransom, you vowed to slit every one of our throats. And yet, you spared me. Why?"

"I admit respect for any man who masters a wild beast. No doubt Hercules favors you. I am not fool enough to kill a man under his protection. Whether the two of you be drowned in the high tide or miraculously saved is not for me to say."

Caesar sighed, as if regretting to admit he harbored a shred of humanity.

"I suppose I take a keen interest in your future, Heraclio the Lion Tamer. You've gone from Numidian mercenary to champion gladiator to pirate captain to prisoner of war. I wonder where you will pop up next."

We were dispatched to Dead Man's Rock. The slick surface titled at an angle. I was afraid I would slip into the sea. One of the sailors tossed a key and a water flask at us. Heraclio caught the flask. I reached for the key but it bounced out of my grasp. Antigone stretched out in a lightning-fast movement to catch it in her mouth. I unlocked my wrists and ankles then handed it to Heraclio.

We watched the ship head up the coast toward Ostia. The water rose quickly around us. I couldn't think beyond the slick triangle of rock that was the only object between me and the depths of the angry ocean. In the west, the sun sank behind the hills of Sicily. The stars ruled the sky. The wind picked up. The temperature dropped. My whole body shivered. My teeth chattered. I hugged my knees to my chest. Heraclio wrapped his thick, harry arm around my shoulders.

"It's the Winter Solstice," he noted, gazing up at the stars.

The longest night of the year.

The sea swirled around us. I looked over the edge at the rising water. The raging current tossed up a collection of luminescent fish. Antigone peered at them with delight.

Her skin sprouted glowing spots to match the inner light of these deep-sea creatures.

"Will we die on this rock?" One of those childish questions I was inclined to ask when I was afraid.

"I think not. For now, try to sleep. We will see how things look in the morning."

"I don't know if I can," I admitted.

He squeezed my shoulders comfortingly.

"How did you come to be a slave in the first place?" I asked.

"Same way as anyone, I suppose."

"But, I mean, how old were you?" I felt less afraid when Hercalio was speaking in his deep, soothing voice.

"I was born in Numidia fifty-two years ago," he began. "My family belonged to a tribe of farmers and herders. At that time, Numidia was still an independent kingdom ruled by King Gauda. Life there was peaceful. The Romans had allowed our kings to continue ruling—as long as they supplied Rome with an abundance of grain and sent our young men to fight in Rome's foreign wars."

"When I was eighteen, Gauda died. A civil war broke out between his two sons, vying for the role of king. The Roman Senate decided the outcome would impact their interests, so they sent General Sulla to back the brother named Hiempsal. But infighting within the Roman military resulted in General Marius backing the other brother, Hierbas."

"I volunteered to fight in the auxiliary cavalry on the side of Hierbas and Marius. Seven years later, my side was defeated. Rome backed Hiempsal as the new King of Numidia. I was taken as a prisoner of war, sold into slavery, and found myself a gladiator for the House of Batiatus. You know the rest."

"Why did you run away?" I asked, to keep him talking.

"Why does any slave run away?" he shrugged. "To regain my freedom."

"I mean, what motivated you to run when you did?"

"I had served Batiatus as a gladiator for ten years and as Doctore of his ludus for twenty. It was the eve of my fiftieth birthday. I asked my gods, Baal and Tenet, to guide me in how I might proceed for the remainder of my life. Their answer was clear. I must return to my homeland a free man. I asked Spartacus, Crixus, and Oneaumais to join me. But they all had children. It wouldn't have been worth it to them. Unlike Spartacus, I lacked a Dionysian prophesy that would inspire others to follow me."

He looked at me seriously.

"Spartacus gets all the glory," he said. "But if not for your Mater's prophesy, none of this would have happened."

As soon as he said it, I could see that he was right. The Spartacus Revolt would never have happened if it hadn't been for news of Mater's Prophesy spreading throughout the slave communities of Italy. I hoped she still lived to carry on the struggle.

"You must sleep," Heraclio said. "I will make sure you do not slip into the sea. At dawn, we will swim to Sicily."

I curled up on my side, knees and elbows to my chest like the corpse of a newborn in a funeral urn.

28

Dawn

Heraclio shook my shoulder. I sat up. The eastern horizon had brightened from inky black to deep purple.

"Eat." He held out a handful of seaweed.

I plucked a few strands and dangled them into my mouth. They tasted salty, green, and fishy. Antigony snatched a long strand and began a process of swallowing that would take her all day. Her skin shimmered from murky black to jade-green.

Heraclio handed me the flask. "Drink."

I gulped greedily. The sun announced itself as a blood red line above the Italian shoreline. In the west, a flash of gold beamed out from Athena's shield. With the shackle key in my hand, I lay on my belly and reached down to dip it into the icy water.

"Athena, protector of seafarers, please soothe the waters between here and your Temple, that my friend Heraclio the Lion Tamer and I may swim safely to your shores. If you protect us from drowning, I promise to lay this key at your feet."

Heraclio grasped my shoulders and looked sternly into my eyes.

"Can you make it?" he asked.

I nodded.

"Aim for the shield. I'll follow. If you get tired, I'll keep you afloat."

"But what about the whirlpool of Scylla? And the jaws of Charybdis?"

"That is a myth told by sailors not skilled enough to harness the tidal streams to their advantage."

I dove into the waves. Each time my face bobbed above the surface, my eyes fixed on Athena's shield. I forgot that the water was freezing cold. That my body was parched to the bone. I thought only of the next wave as I scrambled across it.

I swam until my palms hit sand and my knees scraped across a bed of broken seashells. With my last bit of energy, I half-crawled, half-dragged myself onto the beachhead and lay on my back with my eyes closed. The sand was warm, the sunlight soothing.

Heraclio crawled up beside me, panting with exhaustion.

"We made it, my girl."

Basking in the sweet, welcoming breeze of the Sicilian coast, I drifted into oblivion.

29

Afternoon

I awoke to find Heraclio gone. He had drawn three arrows in the sand.

One pointed south along the coast, with the word MESSINA.

The second pointed out to sea, labelled ITALY.

The third pointed inland: ATHENA.

In the center he had placed one of the coins from around his neck. A gold Ostrich.

Antigone had turned seaweed green and wound herself around a piece of driftwood that lay beside me. I picked it up. She spiraled around my wrist, revealing the object she had been hugging.

One of the votive dolls I had put out to sea.

I climbed the rolling hills inland, my sights set on Athena. At her huge sandaled foot, I fell to my knees, kissed the nail of her big toe, and gazed up at her majestic face. I lay the key on a marble altar between her feet.

"Thank you for seeing Hercalio and me safely to Sicily. I offer you this key to honor your love of freedom."

A small Temple was nestled into the side of the slope, about a hundred feet below the statue. Government signs posted on columns at the entrance announced that anyone caught harboring a fugitive from the Army of Spartacus would be buried alive.

Inside, I was greeted by two priestesses who hugged a blanket around my shoulders, escorted me into the cella, sat me on a pallet near the fire, and served me a chalice of warm fig wine.

"I'm Violeta," the younger priestess told me.

"Iris," the older one said.

"Kalysta."

They seemed to understand that my gratitude was too deep for words. I offered my votive doll to the sacred fire then lay exhausted on the pallet.

I was brutalized by nightmares animating variations of the bloody massacre on the beach. The head of Spartacus mounted on a pike. Mater, crying black tears over his headless corpse. Simon, chained by the neck in a line of six thousand prisoners, shuffling down Via Annia toward Rome. The sky-blue rowboat, bashed against Dead Man's Rock and sucked into the whirlpool of Scylla. Everyone I had ever cared for, crushed between the jaws of Charybdis. Me, trapped inside the treasure chest on the ocean floor. Antigone, her skin peeling off in strips, swimming aimlessly out to sea. Gaius Julius Caesar at the bow of a ship, cackling with an evil laugh and drinking a toast to his glorious future.

In the morning, the priestesses greeted me with a plate of sliced quince, soft cheese, and bread.

"You don't have to tell us anything," Iris assured me.

"You can stay as long as you like," Violeta added.

"Gratitude."

I handed them the ostrich coin. I was dying to ask—and at the same time did not want to know—if they had heard news of the massacre and what had become of the captives.

Instead, I asked for a broom to sweep around the altar. I washed Athena's bronze feet with libations of wine. Antigone's skin shimmered like gold.

For hours, I sat straddling the foot of the goddess, my back against her ankle, gazing across the Strait. I could not bear to dwell on the past. I could bring forth no vision of the future. Each day I returned to my place on the statue, lost in a contemplative trance that lasted from dawn till dusk.

I wondered if Spartacus had really been slain. If Mater had escaped to the mountains. Or died at his side. Or been taken prisoner. And what had become of Tavia and Plutus. Of Apicius and the kitchen staff. Of Thallus, Anthusa, Ursula, and Marius.

I wondered if Lucius was still fighting for his homeland. Or lay heroically slain on a battlefield. Or was safely settled with his clan in a new village.

If Felix and Vitalio had fared well in Pompeii. Or been identified as runaways, tortured, and executed.

I thought of Simon . . .

I marveled that the Spartacus Revolt had happened at all. That it had lasted close to three years. I wondered if anyone in the future would believe sixty thousand slaves could accomplish what we had achieved.

I imagined famous writers, recounting their own versions of the Slave Revolt that had brought shame upon so many generals and was remarkable for the number of battles Rome had lost. Perhaps even now men like Cicero were chronicling a rebellion they knew nothing about.

The Temple had a library in an antechamber behind the cella, crowded with shelves of dusty scrolls. The priestesses told me they had been written and collected by generations of priestesses, dating back a thousand years. They encouraged me to write my own memoir of the Revolt.

"But I was just a girl when it started. I'm still a girl. I'm not a warrior. I can't tell a heroic, epic tale of heroes and battles and martyrs. I cannot, as Homer did, 'Sing of the Muses and Apollo.' My story is merely about my friends. My fears. My family. My failed efforts."

"That is why you must tell it. The Romans will write of battles won and lost. Military tactics. Heroes and martyrs. Winners and losers. Only a girl can tell the story of the Spartacus Revolt as lived by a girl. Not just any girl. A gladiator's daughter. A priestess's daughter. You were there from the beginning. You lived it. You saw the human side of Spartacus. The father. The husband. The Thracian shepherd who tried to change the world."

I sighed heavily. "I'll think about it."

My Hope vial had run dry. I wandered the hills, gathering violets, sweet clover, and lilacs. Violeta showed me how to crush the petals with a mortar and pestle and stew them in olive oil over hot coals in a copper pot. I refilled my vial with this elixir of home brewed Hope. Antigone insisted on being blessed with a drop on the top of her head. Her skin transformed to a serene green, sprinkled with pale lavender spots.

30

Late December

One morning, sitting on Athena's foot, I watched as a small craft drifted to shore. A figure stepped into the surf, dragged the vessel onto the beach, and collapsed in the sand.

It was late afternoon before the figure stood and looked from one end of the beach to the other. Then across the Strait. The traveler headed inland across the rolling hills. Dusk fell. I returned to the cella to eat with my priestess guardians.

I lay on my pallet, too restless to sleep. I went out to sit on the cool marble steps of the Temple entrance. A dark figure made its way up the hill. I was not afraid. Pilgrims often arrived in the night and slept on the temple steps.

As the stranger approached, I saw a mass of dark curls. My heart wobbled in my chest. Antigone's tail flicked excitedly. Could it be Simon? But that was impossible. How could he have survived the massacre?

The closer he came, the more certain I felt it was him. I could hardly believe my eyes.

Simon stood at the bottom of the steps. Our eyes met.

"My dear friend," he said.

"Is it really you?"

I threw my arms around him. He hugged back. I could feel the dampness of his tears on my cheek. Antigone stretched out from my neck to nuzzle his earlobe.

We pulled back to look at each other.

"You must be starving," I said.

"I am."

"Wait here."

Inside, Iris and Violeta were still sleeping. I arranged a few olives and figs on a plate and poured a cup of warm fig wine. While Simon sat on the steps eating, I found an extra pallet and blanket in the storage room and lay it on the perron between the entrance columns. We said goodnight and I went back to my own pallet.

In the morning I introduced Simon to Iris and Violeta. They didn't ask where he'd come from or why. We walked up the hill to Athena and sat straddling her giant feet, our backs against her ankles.

I told him how I had noticed the red crest. Then the transport boats full of soldiers. How I had swum out to warn Spartacus, been swept off the boat, pulled out by soldiers, taken to the flagship, and locked in the brig with Heraclio. And how we had been left to die on Deadman's Rock. And swam to Sicily.

"What about you?" I asked.

"I ran to the south end of the beach to announce the pirate ships had arrived," he began. "By the time I got there, soldiers were storming the beach. Everyone ran for the hills. The soldiers overtook them, cutting them down as easily as a scythe, threshing stalks of wheat. I went to our secret cove. From behind the rocks, I saw Spartacus dive from his boat. I saw the boat tip and the treasure tumble into the sea."

"Then I saw you being handed up the side of the flagship. I kept my eyes on it, hoping to discover what they would do with you. I figured if they threw you overboard, I would take our boat out to rescue you."

"At dusk, the soldiers took their longboats back to the ships. Or returned to the roads at either end of the beach that led to their garrisons. Thousands of prisoners, chained neck to neck, were marched beside them.

"Did you see my Mater and Pater?" I asked. "Or Tavia? Or Plutus? Or anyone we know?"

"I couldn't tell. They were too far away. After dark, I ventured out to look for survivors among the tens of thousands of bodies that covered the ground from the beachhead to the cliffs. I did not find a single living soul. Before dawn I returned to the cove. I watched as the soldiers counted the bodies, marking tallies on wax tablets."

"Did you find anyone you recognized among the dead bodies? Caesar claims Spartacus was struck down and killed by six men."

"You don't understand. It was dark. The bodies were piled on top of each other three deep. It was impossible to recognize anyone."

"How did you make it here?" I asked.

"Night fell and I slept in our boat. When I awoke, the ships were gone. I had no idea what they had done with you. I set out to sea, aiming for the shield of Athena.

Halfway across, I lost an oar when a wave washed over me. All I could do was drift, hoping the tide would pull me toward Sicily."

I closed my eyes, soaking up the heat of the sun-warmed statue. We sat in silence for a long time. There was nothing more to say. No amount of talk could undo the horrific conclusion to our three-year struggle.

I was too afraid to leave the area of the Temple and statue. Iris and Violeta said my presence would look less suspicious if I wore the robes of a priestess. They assured me I need not take vows but that it was the safest way for me to stay there without calling attention to myself.

Simon went into town to seek out the Jewish community. He was welcomed into a Yeshiva, where Jewish boys are taught to read Hebrew and study Torah. They offered him room and board in exchange for tutoring the boys who struggled with their lessons.

In the evening, he walked up the hill to sit with me on the feet of Athena. We watched the eastern sky change colors as the sun set behind us.

"There were signs posted on every building, announcing the defeat of Spartacus," he told me.

Simon had learned that the army of Crassus had been aided by the arrival of a General nicknamed the Butcher Boy, whose legion had stormed the beach from the south road. Together they were expected to be named consuls for the coming year.

"I heard rumors that several hundred survivors have taken refuge in the mountains," Simon added. "The Romans have no interest in pursuing them. They believe it would only serve to call attention to them. Better to let everyone believe the Spartacus Revolt is good and dead."

I liked to think Mater was among the survivors. Maybe even serving as their new leader.

"Do you want to hear what they've done with the six thousand prisoners?" he asked hesitantly.

I nodded.

"Every last one, including women and children, has been crucified. Crassus lined both sides of the Via Appia between Capua and Rome with six thousand prisoners of the Spartacus war nailed to wooden crosses. Everyone who travels the road must look upon the suffering faces of the followers of Spartacus. He ordered that they be left to rot on the crosses until the vultures have picked their bones clean."

I had heard of crucifixion as a favorite method of execution for slaves and foreigners but had never seen it with my own eyes.

Neither of us spoke for a long time.

"I met a couple of people at a café who are interested in meeting me there to discuss philosophy," he added brightly.

We sat there looking across the Strait until night fell.

"It's a full moon," I noted.

"Want to go out in our boat?" Simon suggested.

We strolled down to the beach and pulled our rowboat into the surf. When we had rowed out for a while, we lifted our paddles and allowed ourselves to drift.

"It's strange to think that, because I was captured by Caesar—what I thought was the worst thing that has ever happened to me—I was spared from being slaughtered on the beach," I told him.

"The Stoics say when something bad happens, it often results in something good happening later. Something entirely unexpected, that never would never have come about if the bad thing hadn't—directly or indirectly—led to it. It doesn't make the bad thing any less bad. It's just a fact of life that wonderful things can inadvertently emerge from terrible things."

"You mean everything happens for a reason?"

"Not necessarily. More that there will always be unforeseen consequences."

I thought of the mythical Phoenix, rising from the ashes of its own destruction.

There, in the waves, clasping hands with Simon, I felt I was finally home. Antigone wrapped herself around our hands as if to seal the bond between us.

It struck me that maybe home isn't a place or even a group of people but something you build. And if you build that home with another person, maybe that person becomes an integral part of it.

Was the now-cold hearth in my parents' village in Thrace a home to them because it once held fires they had built together? A hearth Mater had tended daily with wood chopped by Pater? More than a decade after being forced to abandon it, with no hope of returning, they carried that hearth in their hearts. That was their home. Not the fragile structure of wood in which they had resided.

Maybe the sky-blue rowboat Simon and I had built together would always be my true home, even years after the wood had rotted, the nails buried in sand or carried out to sea. Even if we were again to be separated, I would forever carry in my heart these nights together with Simon in our sky-blue rowboat.

"I got something for you," Simon said. "In the marketplace."

He held out an amulet.

"It's beautiful!" I examined it more closely in the moonlight. An amethyst, engraved with an intaglio of a woman holding a reed up to her chin, as if contemplating what she will write next. "It's Clio!"

The Muse of history.

Antigone sprouted purple spots to match the gem. I turned it in my hand. Etched on the reverse were the words

PERICULOSAM LIBERTATEM

"In a way," he said. "Clio is a sort of messenger in her own right."

As soon as he said it, I knew exactly what he meant.

"Because history is a message from the past!" I blurted out.

He grinned and squeezed my hand.

We rowed to shore and pulled the boat out, storing it in the underbrush. Simon walked me back to the Temple then went into town to sleep at the Yeshiva.

In the *scriptorium*, I lit a lamp and sat at the desk with a quill, papyrus roll, and pot of ink. There, in the shadow of Athena's shield, I began to write:

I sat in my usual spot, my back against the sun-warmed wall of the women's entrance to the public bathhouse. A sign above my head, scrawled in blood-red paint, announced . . . .

Thank you for reading *Athena's Shield.*

If you enjoyed this novel, I encourage you to post a rating and (if you have time) write a brief personal reaction to the story on Amazon. LW

Why Spartacus?

The significance of the Spartacus Slave Revolt to freedom fighters around the world over a period of 2,000 years is attested by its influence on and inspiration to several key historical figures, including: Toussant Louverture, leader of the Haitian slave revolution; the Italian revolutionary Giuseppe Garibaldi; and the Zionist Vladimir Jabotinsky. (Source: Barry Strauss, *The Spartacus War*. New York: Simon & Schuster, 2009.)

Director Spike Lee ended his 1993 biopic *Malcolm X* with an "I am Malcolm X" scene that resonates with the famous "I am Spartacus" scene in the movie *Spartacus* (1960), thus drawing a direct line between the Spartacus Slave Revolt and the Black Power Movement.

For me, as a Jew, the Spartacus Slave Revolt has always resonated with the story of Moses leading the Jews out of slavery in Egypt.

Acknowledgments

Athena's Shield is a work of fiction. For a well-researched, scholarly-but-accessible history of the Spartacus slave revolt, one can do no better than to read ***The Spartacus War*** by **Barry Strauss.**

The following Classics scholars were kind enough to provide feedback on brief passages of *Athena's Shield* that are relevant to their area of expertise. All errors – historical or otherwise -- are entirely my own.

Arlene L Allan, Senior Lecturer in Classics, University of Otago, New Zealand. **Harriet I. Flower,** Professor of Classics, Princeton University. **David Weston Marshall**, Professor Emeritus, Texas Tech University. **Richard P. Martin**, Professor of Classics, Stanford University. **Adrienne Mayor,** Research Scholar, Classics & History & Philosophy of Science, Stanford University.

About the Author

Lizzi Wolf was born in Detroit, Michigan. She holds a B.A. from Oberlin College and a Ph.D. in American Culture from University of Michigan.

Lizzi has taught courses in Film Studies, Popular Culture, and Literature at colleges in Michigan, South Carolina, and Massachusetts.

Her other novels include *Meager Mercies: A novel based on the true story of an 8-year-old boy who spent nine months in Solitary Confinement* (2023) and *The Versailles of Sadness: A Novel of Gothic Psychiatry* (2022). Check out her web page at: Lizziwolf.com.

Sources

In the course of my research for *Athena's Shield,* I read over 100 books by scholars and historians of antiquity, including the following.

Abulafia, David. *The Great Sea: A Human History of the Mediterranean*. New York: Oxford UP, 2011. Print.

Allan, Arlene. *Hermes*. London: Routledge, 2018.

Andrade, Nathanael J. *Syrian Identity in the Greco-roman World.* New York: Cambridge UP, 2013. Print.

Apicius. *Cooking and Dining in Imperial Rome*. Ed. Joseph Dommers Vehling. Trans. Joseph Dommers Vehling. New York: Dover, 1977.

Aurelius, Marcus. *Meditations: A New Translation*. Trans. Gregory Hays. New York: Modern Library, 2003.

Barca, Natale. *Rome's Sicilian Slave Wars: The Revolts of Eunus & Salvius, 136-132 & 105-100 B.C.* Philaselphia: Pen & Sword Military, 2020. print.

Beard, Mary. *Laughter in Ancicent Rome: On Joking, Tickling, and Cracking Up*. Berkeley: U of California Press, 2014. Print.

—. *Pompeii*. London: Profile Books, 2010. Print.

Beard, Mary, John North and Simon Price. *Religions of Rome: Volume I: A History*. Cambridge: Cambridge UP, 1998.

Beattie, Andrew. *The Alps: A Cultural History*. New York: Oxford UP, 2006. print.

—. *The Danube: A Cultural History*. New York: Oxford UP, 2010. print.

Bedoyere, Guy De La. *Gladius: The World of the Roman Soldier*. Chicago: U of Chicago P, 2020. print.

Blauer, Ettagale and Jason Laure'. *Mauritania.* New York: Marshall Cavendish Benchmark, 1997. Print.

Bradley, Keith. *Slavery and Society at Rome.* Cambridge: Cambridge UP, 1994.

Bramshaw, Vikki. *Dionysus: Exciter to Frenzy: A Study of the God Dionysus: History, Myth and Lore.* London: Avalonia, 2013. Print.

Brennan, Chris. *Hellenistic Astrology: The Study of Fate and Fortune.* Denver: Amor Fati, 2017. Print.

Brett, Michael and Elizabeth Fentress. *The Berbers.* Malden, MA: Blackwell, 1996. print.

Budin, Stephanie Lynn. *Artemis.* London: Routledge, 2016. Print.

Crawford, Michael H. *Roman Republican Coinage, Vol. II: Studies, Plates and Indexes.* New York : Cambridge UP, 2019. print.

Crawford, Michael. *Roman Republican Coinage, Vol 1: Introduction and Catalogue.* New York: Cambridge UP, 2019. print.

D'Amato, Raffaele. *Republican Roman Warships 509-27 BC.* Oxford: Osprey, 2015.

D'Ambra, Eve. *Roman Women.* Cambridge: Cambridge UP, 2007.

Davies, W.D. and Louis, Eds. Finkelstein. *The Cambridge History of Judaism, Volume Two: The Hellenistic Age.* New York: Cambridge UP, 1989. print.

de Souza, Philip. *Piracy in the Graeco-Roman World.* New York: Cambridge UP, 1999. Print.

Deacy, Susan. *Athena.* New York: Routledge, 2008.

Dougherty, Carol. *Prometheus.* London: Routledge, 2006.

Eckert, Alexandra, Ed. and Thein, Alexander, Ed. *Sulla: Politifcs and Reception.* Berlin: De Gruyter, 2021. Print.

Everitt, Anthony. *Cicero: The Life and Times of Rome's Greatest Republican.* New York: Random House, 2001.

Faraone, Christopher A. and F. S. Naiden. *Greek and Roman Animal Sacrifice: Ancient Victims, Modern Observers*. Cambridge: Cambridge UP, 2012.

Farnsworth, Ward. *The Practicing Stoic: A Philosophical User's Manual*. Boston: David Gordine, 2018. print.

Fischer, Lorenz Andreas. *The Alps: High Mountains in Motion*. teNeues, n.d. print.

Flower, Harriet I. *The Dancing Lares & the Serpent in the Garden: Religion at the Roman Street Corner*. Princeton: Princeton UP, 2017. print.

Fol, Alexander and Fol, Valeria. *The Thracians*. Tangra TanNakRa, 2008. print.

Fol, Alexander and Ivan Marazov. *Thrace & the Thracians*. New York: St. Martin's, 1977. print.

Fowler, W. Warde. *The Roman Festivals of the Period of the Republic: An Introduction to the Calendar and Religious Events of the Roman Year*. Pantianos Classics, 1899. print.

Freeman, Philip. *Julius Caesar*. New York: Simon & Schuster, 2008.

Gager, John G. *Curse Tablets and Binding Spells from the Ancient World*. New York : Oxford UP, 1992. print.

—. *Moses in Greco-Roman Paganism*. Atlanta: Society of Biblical Literature, 1972. print.

Hamilton, Edith and Jim Tierney. *Mythology: Timeless Tales of Gods and Heroes*. New York: Black Dog & Leventhal, 2017. print.

Hoddinott. *The Thracians*. New York: Thames and Hudson, 1981. Print.

Horbury, William, Ed., W.D., Ed. Davies and John, Ed. Sturdy. *The Cambridge History of Judaism, Volume Three: The Early Roman Period*. New York: Cambridge UP, 1999. print.

Horsted, William. *The Numidians: 300 BC-AD300*. Oxford: Osprey, 2021.

Hunt, Peter. *Ancient Greek and Roman Slavery*. Hoboken: Wiley Blackwell, 2018. Print.

Jacob, H.E. *Six Thousand Years of Bread: Its Holy and Unholy History*. Garden City, NY: Lyons, 1944. print.

Joshel, Sandra R. and Lauren Hackworth Petersen. *The Material Life of Roman Slaves*. Cambridge: Cambridge UP, 2014.

Keay, John. *The Spice Route: A History*. Berkeley: U of California P, 2006. print.

Keegan, Peter. *Graffiti in Antiquity*. London: Routledge, 2014. Print.

Kindstedt, Paul S. *Cheese and Culture: A History of Cheese and Its Place in Western Civilzation*. White River Junction, VA: Chelsea Green, 2012. print.

King, Anthony. *Roman Gaul and Germany*. U of California P, 1990. print.

Klavans, Zander H. *Handbook of Ancient Greek & Roman Coins*. Palham, AL: Whitman, 2020. Print.

Kolb, Anne, Ed. *Roman Roads: New Evidence - New Perspectives*. Berlin: De Gruyter, 2021. Print.

Landels, John G. *Music in Ancient Greece and Rome*. New York: Routledge, 1999.

Lapatin, Kenneth. *Luxus: The Sumptuous Arts of Greece and Rome*. Los Angeles: J. Paul Getty Museum, n.d. print.

Leon, Harry J. *The Jews of Ancient Rome, Updated Edition*. Peabody, MA: Hendrickson, 1995. print.

Mackay, Christopher. *The Breakdown of the Roman Republic: From Oligarchy to Empire*. New York: Cambridge UP, 2009.

MacLachlan, Bonnie. *Women in Ancient Rome: A Sourcebook*. London: Bloomsbury, 2013. Print.

Macleod, Roy. *The Library of Alexandria: Centre of Learning in the Ancient World*. London: I.B. Taurus, 2000.

Manco, Jean. *Blood of the Celts: The New Ancestral Story*. London: Thames and Hudson, 2015.

Manoledakis, Manolis, et al. *Essays on the Archaology and Ancient History of the Black Sea Littoral*. Paris: Peeters, 2018. print.

Marshall, David Weston. *Ancient Skies: Constellation Mythology of the Greeks*. New York: Countryman Press, 2018.

Martindale, Charles, Ed. *Ovid Renewed: Ovidian Influences on literature and art from the Middle Ages to the Twentieth Century*. New York: Cambridge UP, 1988. print.

Matyszak, Philip. *24 Hours in Ancient Rome: A Day in the LIfe of the People Who Lived There*. London: Michael O'Mara, 2017.

Mayor, Adrienne. *Gods and Robots: Myths, Machines, and Ancient Dreams of Technology*. Princeton: Princeton UP, 2018.

—. *The First Fossil Hunters: Dinosaurs, Mammoths, and Myth in Greek and Roman Times*. Princeton: Princeton UP, 2000. Print.

McDonough, Yona Zeldis. *Where Were the Seven Wonders of the Ancient World?* New York: Penguin Workshop, 2020. Print.

Meijer, Fik. *The Gladiators: History's Most Deadly Sport*. New York : Thomas Dunne, 2003. print.

Mendelssohn, Sidney. *The Jews of Africa*. 1920.

Miles, Richard. *Carthage Must Be Destroyed: The Rise and Fall of an Ancient Civilization*. New York: Penguin, 2010.

Morris, Edwin T. *Fragrance: The Story of Perfume from Cleopatra to Chanel*. New York: E.T. Morris, 1984. print.

Nutton, Vivian. *Ancient Medicine (2nd Edition)*. London: Routledge, 2013. Print.

O'Connor, George. *Athena: Grey-Eyed Goddess*. New York: Neal Porter, 2010. print.

—. *Hephaistos: God of Fire*. New York: First Second, 2019. print.
O'Shea, Stephen. *The Alps: A Human History from Hannibal to Heidi and Beyond.* New York: Norton, 2017. print.
Ovid. *Fasti: A New translation*. Trans. Anne and Peter Wiseman. Oxford: Oxford UP, 2011.
Panetta, Marisa Ranieri, Ed. *Pompeii: The History, Life and Art of teh Buried City*. Milan: White Star Publishers, 2012. print.
Plautus. *Four Comedies*. Trans. Erich Segal. Oxford: Oxford UP, 1996.
Raven, Susan. *Rome in Africa*. New York: Routledge, 1993.
Rawson, Beryl. *Children and Childhood in Roman Italy*. Oxford: Oxford UP, 2003.
Richardson, John S. *The Romans in Spain*. Oxford: Blackwell, 1996.
Roller, Duane W. *Empire of the Black Sea: The Rise and Fall of the Mithridatic World*. New York: Oxford UP, 2020. print.
Sallust. *Cataline's Conspiracy, The Jugurthine War, Histories*. Trans. William W. Batstone. Oxford: Oxford UP, 2010.
SalzGeber, Jonas. *The Little Book of Stoicism: Timeless Wisdom to Gain Resiliance, Confidence, and Calmness*. Jonas Salzgeber, 2019.
Sampson, Gareth C. *The Collapse of Rome: Marius, Sulla & the First Civil War*. Barnsley: Pen & Sword , 2020.
Schwartz, David G. *Roll the Bones: The HIstory of Gambling, Casino Edition*. Las Vegas: Winchester, 2013. print.
Seaford, Richard. *Dionysos*. London: Routledge, 2006.
Sekunda, Nick and Angus McBride. *Republican Roman Army 200-104 BC*. London: Osprey, 1996.
Sofroniew, Alexandra. *Household Gods: Prive Devotion in Ancient Greece and Rome*. Los Angeles: J. Paul Getty Museum, 2015. print.

Stafford, Emma. *Herakles*. London: Routlege, 2012.

Stern, Karen B. *Writing on the Wall: Graffiti and the Forgotten Jews of Antiquity*. Princeton: Princeton UP, 2018. Print.

Steves, Rick. *Sicily*. Avalon Travel, 2019.

Storrie, Paul D. and Steve Kurth. *Hercules: The Twelve Labors: A Greek Myth*. Minneapolis: Lerner, 2007. Print.

Strauss, Barry. *The Spartacus War*. New York: Simon & Schuster, 2009.

Taieb-Carlen, Sarah. *The Jews of North Africa: From Dido to De Gaulle*. Lanham, MA: UP of America, 2010. Print.

Tanner, George. *Stoicism: A Detailed Breakdown on Stoicism Philosophy and Wisdom from the Greats*. George Tanner, 2017. Print.

Terrence. *The Comedies*. Trans. Peter Brown. Oxford: Oxford UP, 2006.

Todd, Malcolm. *The Early Germans (2nd Edition)*. Malden, MA: Blackwell, 2004. print.

Toynbee, J.M.C. *Animals in Roman Life & Art*. London: Thames & Hudson, 1973. Print.

Walson, J. Michael and Marianne McDonald, *The Cambridge Companion to Greek and Roman Theatre*. Cambridge: Cambridge UP, 2007.

Webber, Chris. *The Gods of Battle: The Thracians at War, 1500 BC - AD 150*. South Yorkshire, UK: Pen & Sword Military, 2011. print.

Wright, M. R. . *Cosmology in Antiquity*. London: Routledge, 1995.

Yegul, Fikret. *Bathing in the Roman World*. New York: Cambridge UP, 2010. Print.

That's my story and I'm stickin' to it!

MEDUSA BOOKS

(June/2/2023)